Rowe is a paranormal star!" ~J.R. Ward

Praise for Darkness Unleashed

"Once more, award winning author Stephanie Rowe pens a winner with *Darkness Unleashed,* the seventh book in her amazing Order of the Blade series…[an] action-packed, sensual story that will keep you perched on the edge of your seat, eagerly turning pages to discover the outcome…one of the best paranormal books I have read this year." ~Dottie, Romancejunkies.com

Praise for Forever in Darkness

"Stephanie Rowe has done it again. The Order Of The Blade series is one of the best urban fantasy/paranormal series I have read. Ian's story held me riveted from page one. It is sure to delight all her fans. Keep them coming!" ~ Alexx Mom Cat's Gateway Book Blog

Praise for Darkness Awakened

"A fast-paced plot with strong characters, blazing sexual tension and sprinkled with witty banter, *Darkness Awakened* sucked me in and kept me hooked until the very last page." ~ Literary Escapism

"Rarely do I find a book that so captivates my attention, that makes me laugh out loud, and cry when things look bad. And the sex, wow! It took my breath away… The pace kept me on the edge of my seat, and turning the pages. I did not want to put this book down… *[Darkness Awakened]* is a must read." ~ D. Alexx Miller, Alexx Mo

one of the best romances I have read. I can't wait till it comes out and I can tell the world about it." ~Sharon Stogner, Love Romance Passion

"*No Knight Needed* is contemporary romance at its best....There was not a moment that I wasn't completely engrossed in the novel, the story, the characters. I very audibly cheered for them and did not shed just one tear, nope, rather bucket fulls. My heart at times broke for them. The narrative and dialogue surrounding these 'tender' moments in particular were so beautifully crafted, poetic even; it was this that had me blubbering. And of course on the flip side of the heart-wrenching events, was the amazing, witty humour....If it's not obvious by now, then just to be clear, I love this book! I would most definitely and happily reread, which is an absolute first for me in this genre." ~Becky Johnson, Bex 'N' Books

"*No Knight Needed* is an amazing story of love and life...I literally laughed out loud, cried and cheered.... *No Knight Needed* is a must read and must re-read." ~Jeanne Stone-Hunter, My Book Addiction Reviews

Inferno of Darkness

ISBN-10: 098865668X

ISBN-13: 978-0-9886566-8-0

For further information, please contact Stephanie@ stephanierowe.com

ACKNOWLEDGEMENTS

Special thanks to my beta readers, who always work incredibly hard under tight deadlines to get my books read. I appreciate so much your willingness to tell me when something doesn't work! I treasure your help, and I couldn't do this without you. Hugs to you all!

There are so many to thank by name, more than I could count, but here are those who I want to called out specially for all they did to help this book come to life: Alencia Bates, Jean Bowden, Shell Bryce, Kelley Currey, Holly Collins, Ashley Cuesta, Denise Fluhr, Valerie Glass, Christina Hernandez, Heidi Hoffman, Jeanne Hunter, Rebecca Johnson, Dottie Jones, Janet Juengling-Snell, Deb Julienne, Bridget Koan, Felicia Low, Phyllis Marshall, D. Alexx Miller, Jodi Moore, Judi Pflughoeft, Emily Recchia, Kasey Richardson, Karen Roma, Caryn Santee, Julie Simpson, Summer Steelman, Nicole Telhiard, Linda Watson, and Denise Whelan.

And lastly, thank you to Pete Davis at Los Zombios for another fantastic cover, and for all his hard work on the technical side to make this book come to life, and for the most amazing website. Mom, you're the best. It means so much that you believe in me. I love you. Special thanks also to my amazing, beautiful, special daughter, who I love more than words could ever express. You are my world, sweet girl, in all ways.

DEDICATION

This book is dedicated to the Ladies and Gents of the Blade at the Order of the Blade Reader's group on Facebook. Thanks for the support, the friendship, and for sharing your love of all things Order. You all inspire me on so many levels.

You guys rock!

INFERNO
OF
DARKNESS

THE ORDER OF THE BLADE

STEPHANIE ROWE

CHAPTER ONE

In the beginning, many centuries ago...

Calydon warrior Dante Sinclair braced himself against a tree, unable to hold himself up any longer. Sweat streamed down his lacerated back. His muscles shook with exhaustion. His mangled foot was getting worse, the poison leaching its way up his leg, contamination even he could not heal. The black streaks were like angry webs branching along his flesh, destroying more cells each day.

He thought briefly of summoning Rohan, the one man on this forsaken earth he trusted, the one who had survived hell with him for over a hundred years, but he dismissed the notion the moment it crossed his mind. They'd had an agreement, and they would both stand by it. He'd let the poison take him before he'd call Rohan away from what he needed to do. But hell, he hadn't expected this.

Dante's good leg gave out and he slithered down the tree, the rough bark tearing at his open wounds as he landed on the ground. Swearing, he let his head fall back against the trunk, closing his eyes for a moment.

Not to rest.

Never to rest.

To listen. To focus. To track.

There was one man left to kill. But even as he thought it, a whisper of hope rippled through him. What if he didn't have to kill the one who was left? What if Louis could be the one to help him rebuild? What if…

No. There was no chance. He had to stay focused. He had to kill Louis. He knew he would have to. And once he had done that, he could die. The legacy his father had twisted and mutilated into such darkness would finally be destroyed.

Summoning strength that he shouldn't still have, Dante reached out with his preternatural senses, searching for that telltale vibration he'd been tracking for the last three months. The acrid scent of blood. The cold vibration of evil. The heavy weight of ruthlessness and death. The tainted trail was all that remained of the legendary heroes of the Order of the Blade, the elite group of Calydon warriors who had been created to protect innocents from rogue Calydons, from the demons that turned good men into monsters. That was the mission of the Order, but his father had corrupted it into pure evil that did not deserve to exist, twisting his team into warriors who were beyond scum, fraudulent heroes who deserved an inglorious, dishonorable death. Warriors his father had trained and elevated to glory. The warriors who Dante was almost finished eliminating.

Only one remained alive, the one that Dante had kept for last, hoping that warrior would be worthy, that Dante would be able to spare him. But Louis's trail had become dark and evil, and Dante knew there was nothing left of the man he had once known. Weary with the weight of what he had to do, Dante reached out with his senses to locate the last of his prey.

For a moment, he couldn't sense Louis, and panic flooded him. The poison wouldn't let him live long enough to start the search from scratch. He had to find the bastard now. Frantic, he sprang to his feet, adrenaline chasing away the pain and exhaustion as he spun around, sending out pulses of energy in every direction. When had he lost the trail? Had he been too exhausted to notice when he lost it? Swearing, he went still, holding his palms face up, as if in supplication to the powers that had fueled the Order, the powers that should still answer to him despite his repudiation of the entity.

A dark, circulating energy surged through him, so intense that he shouted in pain. He dropped to his knees, bracing his hands on the earth, screaming as a thousand shocks knifed through him ruthlessly. With a roar of fury, he summoned all his energy and tried to shield himself from the assault, but he could do nothing to block it. Just an endless circle of pain and hell and—

It stopped.

Gasping for breath, Dante bowed his head, struggling to find strength in his beleaguered body. What the hell had that been?

There was a sudden pulse of energy through him again, only this time, it was warm and powerful. Calling him. Summoning him. His head jerked up, and his gaze went directly to the towering mountain range to the south. Snow caked the summit, and a spiral of black smoke spewed from the highest peak. But his attention was drawn halfway down the northwest side, where the forest was thick and the snow had been replaced by lush vegetation. There. *There.* Something in that spot was summoning him. Something violent. Something powerful. Something...steel. It was a weapon. Not his, not the ones branded onto his forearms that were his to call. A weapon he didn't know, but he could tell it was the same energy that had attacked him moments ago. It had attacked, and then summoned him. Had it been testing him? Deciding whether he was worthy?

Was it the sword that had been haunting his dreams for the last few weeks? Was the image that he'd been imagining actually *real*?

He lurched to his feet, studying the spot he'd targeted. An image flashed in his mind of a sword. Just a faint blurry image that was more of a sense than an actual picture. Calling to him. Demanding he go to it, to that spot, to where it was waiting for him. The urge to respond to the summons was surreal, a command so powerful that he actually took a step. And then another. And then—

He caught the ripple of feminine energy mingled with the sword. A woman.

Dante stopped dead, sifting through the information the wind gave him. She was suffering. In pain. But at the same time, dangerous. Deadly. Sensual. Protecting. The guardian of the sword? Conflicting responses rose fast and hard. The need to find her and protect her. The compulsion to track the sword. The need to—

A loud scream ripped through the night, the piercing scream of death, the sound Dante had heard so many times in his life, the sound that still haunted him every minute of every day, the scream that never ceased in his mind, *ever*.

He knew who caused that kind of suffering. There was only one beast. One creature. One being that did not even deserve to be called a man. A Calydon of the Order of the Blade. The warrior he'd been hunting. The last of his kind.

Dante was too late, *again*.

With a roar of fury, Dante whirled around and sprinted toward the sound, the relentless, horrifying wail of suffering and pain beyond what any living creature could endure. It seemed to bounce off the sky and plunge right through his flesh. He ran harder, leaping over fallen logs, stumbling each time his mangled foot hit the ground, but he did not slow. He had to stop him. He had to end this before it was too late.

Tonight, the Order of the Blade would be wiped from this earth, and Dante would be able to die, his job finally finished, his father's legacy finally destroyed, his own destiny wiped out.

Zach burst out of the healer's hut, tearing into the night as the screaming pounded in his ears. Horror congealed in his stomach as he saw his sister sprawled in the dirt in the center of the village, slumped at the feet of a massive warrior covered in blood. "Christina!" Around him were a dozen bloodied bodies, and more people screaming as they tried to run away.

"No!" The anguished roar tore from his throat as the warrior raised his arm to the sky, a bloodied Calydon dagger clenched in his fist. His eyes were red, blood red. He'd gone rogue, and targeted Zach's sister.

Bellowing in rage and terror, Zach sprinted across the square toward the enraged Calydon, trying frantically to draw his attention away from his sister. Unnoticed by the rogue, Zach called out his weapons, tapping into the power of a Calydon to harness the weapons that were branded on his forearms. There was a crack and a flash of black light, and then a sai appeared in each hand. He hurled them instantly as the warrior grabbed his sister by the throat and lifted her up.

"Take me, you bastard!" he screamed as both his sai plunged into the warrior's stomach in a one-two-hit of deadly accuracy.

The warrior didn't even flinch. He just spun around to face Zach, tossing Christina aside like a rag doll. Jesus. For him to shrug off that kind of blow, there was only one explanation. The warrior was an Order member, one that had gone rogue. Jesus. A rogue Order member? How could he possibly stop him?

The rogue hurled his weapons so quickly Zach had no time to react, and they hit him in the throat, in the same one-two strike that he'd done. He gagged and fell to his knees, clutching his neck as the warrior roared his victory and called his weapons back. They tore out of Zach's flesh and hurtled through the air back to his hands.

Zach called his own weapons back, but in an unprecedented move he'd never seen before, the warrior grabbed them as they ripped out of his body, keeping them from returning to Zach, and rendering him defenseless.

His eyes still glowing, he spun around and grabbed Zach's sister again.

Gasping as he croaked his protest, Zach tried to crawl, but it was too little, too late. He would never get there in time. Desperation tore through him as he grimly called upon the one other tool at his disposal, the one he had no control over, the one that he would not try to contain today.

Fire erupted instantly from deep within him, spewing off him in all directions. Zach fell to his side, life draining from him as he held up his arm. Flames streamed toward the sky, a hundred feet into the air, as a fireball formed in his palm, spinning faster and faster, growing bigger and bigger as the bastard aimed his knife toward his sister. *Not my sister.* With a sobbing gasp, Zach hurled the fireball.

It slammed into the warrior's chest, and he dropped Christina again, screaming in agony as the flames ignited his flesh. He spun around, fighting the fire as Zach crawled across the blood-soaked earth, focused only on his sister. Her eyes were glazed with pain, but she saw him coming. She stretched her fingers toward him.

Christina. He collapsed once, then shoved himself to his elbows, dragging himself over the dirt. He reached for her, his hand outstretched, as if he could drag her away—

A shadow moved above them, and he looked up as the warrior plunged the dagger toward Christina. Zach lunged forward, throwing himself over her, trying desperately to turn his flames away from her, to stop himself from burning her—

The dagger meant for Christina plunged into his back. Beyond the realm of his consciousness, Zach heard new screams, the cries of children, and deeper fear knifed through him. The children. Had they come out of the healer's hut? Had they abandoned the refuge he'd ordered them not to leave? "No!" With a roar of desperate fury, Zach surged to his feet and slammed another fireball at his assailant. And another. And another. Until they were consumed by a blazing inferno, until Zach could see nothing but orange flames and smoke—

There was a sickening, insane cackle of laughter, and then the smoke parted, revealing the face of his assailant. His eyes glowed red with the light of the demon, and Zach went cold with sudden fear. How was the bastard still standing? He grabbed Zach around the throat and hurled him aside. Zach flew through the air and crashed into a boulder, his body shattering from the impact. More screams of innocents being hurt filled the air, wrenching at his insides. Flames poured from his body as he tried to get up, but his body was broken. He couldn't breathe. He couldn't—

"It ends now!" There was a loud cry, and Zach looked up to see a Calydon warrior charging across the square toward the rogue. The warrior was taller than any he'd ever seen, with more muscle. His body was bleeding from a hundred deep gouges. His right foot was blackened and deformed, and yet somehow, he was moving with surreal speed, sprinting through the village. "You die, Louis! You *die*!" With a howl of outrage, the warrior leapt through the air, his body arcing thirty feet above the earth as he hurled his spear.

The rogue spun around to face him, but the spear struck him in the heart before he could throw his dagger. He ripped it out and attacked, and suddenly the earth was shaking from the battle between these two massive warriors. Riveted though he was by the display of strength, Zach tore his gaze off them and searched the square for Christina. He saw her crumpled by the hut of one of the village elders. Anguish tore through him, fueling strength into his devastated body. He lurched to his feet and staggered across the square, collapsing beside her. "Christina," he whispered, his voice torn and raspy from the blow to his throat. There was no response.

No. No. *No!* Zach gathered her in his arms and felt the absence of her spirit instantly. She was dead. "No!" He screamed his grief as he cradled her against his chest, as he felt the weight of her body against him for the last time. Then, he saw two small figures slumped nearby. Two children. White-cold fear knifed through him, horror beyond words. "Liv? Thomas?" he croaked.

No, no, no. It couldn't be. *It couldn't be.* Horror rising to a crescendo, still holding his sister in his arms, he lunged to his feet and ran toward them. He fell to his knees before the tiny bodies lying face down in the dirt. "God, no," he whispered as he gently rolled them over. Staring blankly at him were the faces of his niece and nephew. Dead. His sister. Liv. Thomas. All he had left of his family. *Dead. All dead.*

He threw back his head and screamed.

Dante stood, fighting back grief and regret, as he watched Louis stumble and fall, collapsing for the final time. The great warrior, who had terrorized so many, hit the ground with a thundering crash, his massive body thudding to the earth.

For a moment, Dante said nothing. He just stood there, breath heaving in his chest, leaning on his spear as he fought to stay on his feet, barely aware of the screams of the people in the village, of the thick scent of death surrounding him. All he could do was stare into the face of the man who had saved his life so long ago. His leather pants were torn and bloodied, his chest gaping from Dante's blows, his face contorted with pain.

Louis rolled onto his side, his eyes still rogue red, but there was the faintest streak of the brown they'd once been. "You have returned," he said, his voice rough and raw with the contamination of rogue. "You have come back to the Order."

"I have come back to the Order?" Disgust spewed through Dante at the idea, and he walked over to the one Order member he'd thought might have been worth saving. The man who had saved him from his father's lethal attack. The man who had shown mercy to innocents when Dante's father had not been looking. The man he'd waited until last to kill, wanting, wishing, and naively hoping that he might prove himself worthy. Louis had been kidnapped by the Order only three years before Dante, an eight-year-old mentor to the five-year-old Dante, two young boys thrust into merciless training to turn them into the monsters Dante's father coveted.

Louis had once been his friend, and although he had been corrupted by the power of the Order, Dante had never forgotten who he had once been, and he'd hoped that the human being Louis had once been still remained.

But it had been a lie. The blow that had taken Louis down was the seventeenth direct strike to the heart Dante had landed before he'd succumbed. Seventeen times, Louis had survived, granted one more chance to come back to him, to regain control, to be the man Dante had hoped he could be.

Every time, instead of asking forgiveness, Louis had torn the blade out of his chest, and launched another assault, proving what Dante had known all along: that the Order had to be destroyed. Despite the fact he had begun as a good man, Louis had wound up the same as the others, and he had earned the same fate.

"No, Louis. I have not returned to the Order. I have come back to end it." He pressed the tip of his spear to Louis's throat, his hand trembling around the shaft of his weapon. "I've killed everyone else," he said. "You're the only one left."

Louis's eyes widened, and he coughed, splattering blood across the dirt. "Your father?"

"He was the first one I killed." Dante hardened his voice, refusing to replay that moment in his mind. To his surprise, a small smile curved the corner of Louis's mouth, and his body shuddered, almost as if in relief.

"It's over then," he whispered. "Blackthorn's reign of terror is over."

"Yes." Dante pressed the tip more firmly into Louis's neck, knowing the warrior was moments from death. "And now, you die."

"Then it is your turn," Louis said faintly, coughing as blood began to fill his lungs, his injuries too deep for even a Calydon to heal.

"My turn for what? To die?" Dante laughed softly, not even bothering to look down at his decaying foot, at the poison creeping its way up his leg. "I'm dying anyway. Not at your hands—"

"No!" Louis moved suddenly, so quickly that Dante wasn't prepared to react, and Louis got his hand around Dante's arm. "You cannot die," he rasped out. "You must rebuild the Order. You must make it what it was supposed to be."

Dante wrenched his arm free. "The Order is no more! I will never rebuild—"

"You must! Only Order members can save the innocents." Louis coughed again, and what little strength he'd summoned seemed to bleed from his body as he slumped back onto the earth. "Spare us all, Dante," he whispered. "You have the mark. It is your Order now. It is yours. Make it what it should be." And then he was gone, his eyes gazing blankly at Dante's face.

For a moment, Dante simply stared at the last of his father's legacy. He felt empty. Drained. Finished. "I bear no mark," he said quietly. "I left the Order. It's over." Unwilling to deny Louis honor in death, even after all he'd done at his father's bidding, Dante knelt and brushed his hand over Louis's eyes, closing them. As he did so, he saw a pulsing red mark on the underside of his wrist. A cold wind seemed to knife through him as he slowly turned his arm over to inspect it. It was a symbol of crossed swords embedded in a double circle, the same mark that his father had carried. The mark of the leader of the Order of the Blade.

CHAPTER TWO

Dante went still, horror wrenching through him at the sight of the Order's mark on his flesh. "No," he gritted out. "Your legacy is done, Father. *Done.*" He grabbed his spear to cut the mark out of his wrist—

"You killed him," the whisper was raw and anguished, horrified.

"Bless you. Oh, dear saints, bless you."

"Thank you for coming," said another.

Warily, Dante dragged his gaze away from his wrist. Kneeling before him were dozens of townspeople, many of them still splattered with the blood from the battle. Although Dante had just killed a man, they were all looking at him with a great sense of awe and appreciation. Bowing deeply and whispering repeated murmurs of thanks and blessings, they genuflected, as if Dante was some angel who had arrived to save them.

At the front, was the leader of the town, a man who looked like he'd seen a few battles himself, with grizzled hair and a long scar across the side of his sunken face. "We have tried to stop the rogues," he said. "But we can't. No one can. The Order doesn't come anymore. No one has come in a hundred years. Until you. The Order has returned."

Dante shoved himself to his feet. "The Order is gone,"

he said. "No more." He offered the news freely, knowing that this decimated village needed the hope that the Order's reign of terror was over.

"Gone?" The town leader rose to his feet as the villagers erupted into frenzied whispers. "But it can't be gone! We can't defeat the rogues alone!"

"The Order is poison," Dante replied. "They rape your women. They steal your children. They—"

"They save us!"

"They bring suffering upon you!" Dante called his spear back from Louis. It sailed through the air and vanished into the matching black brand seared on his forearm. How could these people not understand what the Order truly was? How could they hold it in esteem after all his father had made them do?

Dante had lived with the horrors of the Order for so long. Every victim they'd killed still bled through him. He'd seen good men, strong men, brave men come into the Order, and change into monsters. Power did that. Power corrupted. Power destroyed even those like Louis, who had good buried deep within their souls. "It's over." But as Dante looked into the stricken faces of the townspeople, many of whom were still cradling the bodies of those who Louis had slain before Dante had arrived, he felt the deep, deep stab of pain in his own chest. He knew all about the grief of losing people they cared about. He fucking *knew that loss.* "It must be this way—"

"You were too late!" The anguished roar ripped across the courtyard, and a burst of fire billowed through the village square. The townspeople screamed and scattered, leaving Dante to face a young Calydon who was standing a hundred yards away, flames cascading from his body and littering the ground around him.

Dante instantly tensed, prepared to charge the male and hurl him into the nearby river to put out the flames, only to realize just as quickly that the man wasn't *on* fire. He *was* fire. The flames were bleeding from his pores, flickering in his eyes, and coating his skin, but not burning him. His upper body was bare, his clothes hanging in burnt embers. "You fucking bastard," he screamed. "He killed my sister! He killed Liv and Thomas! You were too late!" And then with a roar of outrage, the Calydon called out his weapons with a crack and a flash of black light. A three-pronged sai appeared in each hand, matching the brands on his arms. "You stupid, fucking bastard!"

Then he launched himself at Dante, a roiling ball of fire streaking across the bloody dirt right at him.

"Shit!" Dante called out his spears again with a crack and a flash of black light. "Stand down," he shouted. "I don't want to hurt you." Now that the Order was dead, Dante would never kill again. It was over, this life he'd led for so long.

"You betrayed us!" The warrior screamed. "The Order was supposed to protect her!"

"I'm not the Order!" Dante rapidly assessed the best place to slow the youth down without hurting him, and then hurled his spear. The handle slammed into the warrior's feet and tripped him, bringing him down in a jumble of flames.

He skidded to the earth, and the flames erupted around him, charring the barren dirt. Dante saw then that the warrior was badly injured, barely even able to hold himself up. Townspeople rushed over, dumping buckets of water on him, but the flames grew even stronger as he rolled to his hands and knees, glaring at Dante through hooded eyes. "You stupid bastard," he gritted out. "You were supposed to stop the rogues. The Order was supposed to keep her safe."

His mangled foot throbbing in pain, Dante limped over to the warrior and crouched down so that he was eye level with him. "I know. The Order has failed the people. It betrayed its birthright." He gave no excuses. "That's why it's over."

"Over? No Order?" Outrage darkened the younger warrior's features. He tried unsuccessfully to struggle to his knees, but collapsed onto his chest again. "More will die," he gasped. "More innocents. Like my sister. Like her children. What happens when others fall victim to the *sheva* curse? This is what happens when the Order doesn't do its job. *This!*" He flung a bloodied hand out, and Dante saw he was gesturing to the bodies of a young woman and two small children crumpled in the dirt.

Sudden grief rushed through him, and Dante ground his jaw, fighting to contain his emotions. He knew what would happen without the Order. That was why the Order had been formed, to protect innocents from rogue Calydons. A rogue Calydon was insanely strong, virtually unstoppable, except by those trained to be Order members and gifted with the protection of the Order's trinity of guardian angels. A rogue Order member was the most deadly Calydon of all, as Louis had shown. All Calydons were susceptible to going rogue, but those who met their *sheva,* their soul mate, were destined for a violent, bloody end that could not be stopped...except by those trained to do so. Except by the Order as it had once been. But not the Order as it had become. "I know what happens when Calydons go rogue. I know about the *sheva* destiny," he said quietly. "It is the way of our kind."

Since the birth of their race, the Calydons has been subject to the *sheva* destiny: to meet their soul mate, to be unable to resist sealing their connection through the five bonding stages, and then, once the bond was complete, the male would go rogue and destroy all that mattered to either of them, only to be killed by his mate, who would then kill herself in despair of the loss. There was no way to stop the process once begun, no way to protect against the hell that awaited a Calydon and his mate. No way to stop it, unless one of the parties was killed before the final fate took them...and no one could defeat a rogue Calydon, except the Order, as it had been intended to be.

"It doesn't have to be our way," Zach shouted. "It has to

be stopped! You must stop it!"

"I'm not Order—"

"Yes, you are! I heard the rogue! You're the new leader! What are you going to do about it?"

Dante's jaw tightened. "You know nothing of which you speak."

"I know you're a fucking coward who got here too late." The flames bleeding from the other warrior's body grew higher, towering almost twenty feet into the air. "I'll do it," he snarled. "I'll take over the Order. Give me the fucking mark." His eyes were blazing with orange flames even brighter than the ones still cascading off him, and his body was rigid, flexed with the emotions raging through him.

"No!" Dante shoved the warrior back to the ground. "You'll become that which you rail against even now! You have no idea of the power of the Order. *It will destroy you.*"

"You're wrong." Zach was on his hands and knees now, glowering at Dante. "My family died today. I will *never* forget this moment. I will *never* become that which killed them. *Never.*"

The intensity of the youth's words struck at Dante, and he leaned forward, studying him more carefully. The male had to be in his early twenties, well over a hundred years younger than Dante, just at the front edge of his powers, and yet there was an impressive strength within him. A burning in his eyes. "What's your name?"

"Zach Roderick."

"Take your flames down," Dante commanded, testing him.

Zach stared at him, and the flames grew higher, crackling with anger, grief, and loss. A flame leapt to a nearby hut, and the townspeople leapt into well-practiced action with buckets of water, trying to halt the destruction.

"You're too angry," Dante said grimly, disappointment like a sharp knife digging at him. No one was strong enough to do what he needed. No one. "You can't control yourself. You're exactly the type who will fail. To succeed as Order, you have to be cold and hard, above such human weaknesses as love. You have to be stronger than the call of the *sheva* bond. You aren't what I need. You can't stop yourself now. What would you become under duress?"

"Duress? Fuck that!" Zach lurched to his feet, staggering as he fought to stand, despite the decimation of his body. "My sister and her kids fucking *died* today! You don't think I understand what's at stake? Well, *I do.*"

Dante understood Zach's passion, because he had once been the same way, before he'd seen how dangerous it was, before a hundred years in hell had stripped him of everything but the need to survive. Zach was too angry, grieving too deeply, to be able to focus. This battle was too personal to him. Zach would never be strong enough to resist the lure of power. Dante had seen it too many times. He would not invite another into this world only to have them tear down the innocents he had sworn to save. "No. I can't risk it—"

"Mark me!" The flames seemed to be licking right through Zach's skin, burning from the inside out, so fiercely it was almost as if his skin had become translucent, a thin barrier barely containing the fire raging within him. He grabbed Dante's arm. "I can do this! *I can do it!*"

Dante stared into Zach's eyes, which were literally dancing with flames. The young man was made of fire, a deadly force, but so volatile. Too volatile. He knew what he needed, and it wasn't a warrior who would allow his emotions to control him...or even have the emotions in the first place. "No—"

There is a sword you need.

Dante turned sharply at the rough voice in his head, and saw an old man sitting under a tree at the edge of the village square. "Did you speak to me?" Only Calydons could speak into each other's minds, but the old man sitting there had no brands on his forearms, no mark of a Calydon. But the sword...he'd been dreaming of a sword for weeks, an ancient black sword. Plain. Without any jewels, but always surrounded by swirling mists of a dozen colors. It was the same one he'd seen in his mind before the fight with Louis, the one that had called to him from the mountain. "What do you know about the sword?"

The man looked right at Dante, but didn't acknowledge he had spoken. *The sword is your answer. It is searching for you. Open your mind to it. Let it be your guide.*

Even as the words were still echoing in his mind, Dante felt a sudden, intense call reverberate through him, drawing his attention to the south. The air thickened, and Dante turned around to stare at the mountain in the distance.

He studied the thick green foliage that covered the lower half, and the sparse, raw rock. His gaze narrowed to a fissure on the northwest side, from which heavy, thick steam was rising. *There.* He was suddenly filled with the same certainty as before that the sword he sought was in that location. That was where he needed to go. Was the sword the answer he was seeking? His chance to rebuild the Order of the Blade? Was the sword the weapon that his team would need to defeat the rogues?

Shit, no. What was he thinking? There was no more Order. *No more Order.* He hated his father. He hated the Order. His own emotions burned too fucking deep, and he knew he would be corrupted just as the others had. He would not become that which he had finally destroyed.

The sword is your answer.

He narrowed his eyes, reaching out with his mind, to the voice he didn't recognize. *And what's my question?*

You know what it is.

Dante looked back at the carnage behind him, at Zach, who had collapsed again, lying inert in the shredded earth as his body struggled to repair itself before it was too late.

He surveyed the bodies of so many innocents. His gaze fell upon Louis, who wasn't old enough for his body to disappear immediately. Only extremely old Calydons vanished immediately. Even without the Order, rogues would continue to exist. Innocents would still die. The *sheva* bond would still drag warriors and their soul mates toward a horrific, violent end.

He knew what his question was. His question was how to stop the rogues and protect the innocents without allowing the absolute power of the Order to exist and corrupt. He wanted a way that would end it now. *Is there a way?*

The sword is your answer.

Dante had thought he would be done when Louis was dead. He'd thought his job was over. He'd been ready to let the poison finish its job. But was there one more thing he had to do? Gritting his teeth against the pain in his leg, against the taint of poison spreading through him, he nodded. One more task, and he had very little time to accomplish it. *I'm on my way.*

Beware of the female. She is not as she seems.

At the warning, sudden, intense energy flooded him. An awareness so sharp and sensual he literally froze in place, one foot suspended in the air mid-step. Was he talking about the woman Dante had sensed before?

Son of a bitch. Why was he reacting physically to the mere mention of her? Was she his *sheva*? He quickly looked down at his arms and saw that the black lightning bolt tattoos were still dark, circling his arms from wrist to shoulder. The protective runes he'd spent years developing were intact. If she were his *sheva*, she would not be able to penetrate them.

But he couldn't stop the ripple of apprehension. If she were strong enough to make him respond even through his protections when she was so far away, what would happen when he got closer? He'd never tested the runes before, not to his knowledge.

For a moment, he ground his jaw, staring at the mountain. Was it worth the risk? The call was strong, burning through him, becoming more intense by the moment. But at the same time, he knew he was powerful. If he went rogue, there was no one left on this earth who could stop him now that the Order was gone. He could not afford the *sheva* bond, or the rogue it would turn him into. Rohan had sworn the runes would not fail him, but how did he know? The call of the sword was strong, but he was stronger than it was. He could resist it and walk away—

A sai plunged into the dirt at his feet, missing his toe by a breath. He looked up to see Zach blocking his path, favoring his injured leg, fire raging from him in all directions, like a virtual wall of flame. Somehow, against all logic, Zach had managed to stand up again. His body was trembling violently from the effort, but there he stood, fighting for what he wanted. "This can't happen again," Zach growled. "I'm going to stop it. Give me the mark."

Zach's stance was strong, his muscles flexed, but in his eyes and voice, Dante could feel the depths of the warrior's grief for the losses he had suffered today. Resolution poured through him. The warrior was right. It couldn't happen again. It had to end now. And if that sword was the answer, he was willing to risk the woman who guarded it, and the dark desires that swirled through him at the mere thought of her.

There was no time left to be careful.

The Order was over, and it was time for the last protection to be set in place before he died.

"No," he told Zach. "But I will fix this."

The young warrior's eyes seemed to burn even brighter. "I want to go with you."

"No. You're not ready." Another surge of urgency pushed at him, and Dante thought he caught the faint scent of the woman. Something delicate and light, almost ethereal. His damaged leg pulsed in pain, and he knew there was no more time.

It was now.

Without another word, or another thought, Dante channeled all his energy into his foot, erecting a protective shield around it, like an invisible cast. Gritting his teeth against the pain he knew would still come, he broke into a sprint, exploding through the barren lands, racing toward the sword and the woman who might give him everything he wanted...

...or might try to destroy it all.

He was coming.

Elisha hunched down behind the great rock, her fingers digging into the cold, rough surface of the boulder, her black dress floating in ethereal waves around her calves. For days she'd known he was nearing. She'd felt his presence at the same moment that the sword had located him. He was strong. Courageous. Haunted with dark energies of death, destruction, and terrible things that he'd lived and experienced.

His power was immense, thickening with each step he'd taken closer to them, until it had rolled through her all the way to her core, haunting her during sleep, during waking, during every moment. The last six hours, his energy had been horrifically violent, torn asunder by blood, carnage, death, and so much guilt and anguish that she'd barely been able to breathe. Only by submerging herself into the cold water of the nearby mountain stream had she been able to shield herself from the onslaught of his energy.

She was used to the feelings of darkness and death. She was numb to violence now. But the intensity of his emotions was too much, far beyond what she'd ever experienced. It was terrifying...but at the same time...she raised her face to the crisp air and inhaled deeply, letting his deep, masculine vibration fill her, tempt her, test her...and seduce her.

Seduce. A word that had filled her with revulsion for

centuries. Lust was a concept that had tormented her so many nights. Desire was a lie that ate away at her soul. And yet, while she was surrounded by the encroaching energy of this unknown warrior, those words seemed to morph into something different. Thoughts of being touched in ways she'd never conceived of. Longings for things to be other than they had always been. An awareness of being a woman that didn't make her cringe in fear.

No wonder the sword had chosen him.

And even more reason why she had to stop him.

Elisha looked down at the sharp dagger in her right hand. The blade was black, forged in the fires of the realm of the queen's darkness. Smoke swirled through the blade, visible, yet untouchable, a poison that would destroy any creature, no matter where they were from. Regret filled her, and she tore her gaze away from it. She knew what would happen if she had to use it. Killing didn't begin to describe what the dagger would do. It inflicted the very worst kind of death, a horrific, demon-filled demise that plunged the victim into an eternity of the very worst kind of hell. She had seen creatures cut down by it, and the screams of their suffering would never stop haunting her.

It was all she'd been able to take with her from the realm of the queen's darkness, a tool she prayed fervently she would never use. But if she had to, she would. Some things were more important than mercy.

A stone rattled, and Elisha went still, fading her image until she was barely visible, holding herself on the thin edge between nothingness and reality. Her heart began to hammer in anticipation as the shadows lengthened. He was almost here. *Almost here.*

Longing coursed through her, an ardent, almost uncontrollable need to see him, to know this man she'd been sensing for so long. But even as she inched forward, she sent a whisper out into the air. "Turn back," she said, blowing her words toward him, so that they slid in and out of the trees, riding the wave of the air current. "You do not want this sword." Her whisper echoed again and again, the message finding its way along the airstream toward the man who was approaching.

She felt a flicker in his energy, and she knew he'd heard her. And then, blown back at her, on the pathway that she'd created, came his response, a deep, male voice that reverberated through her like a dangerous symphony of strength and beauty. *Yes, I do. And I'm coming to get it.*

CHAPTER THREE

He wanted her.

There was no way for Dante to deny his physical response to the whispered warning she had sent dancing along the breeze to him. He had no idea who she was, or what she looked like, but her voice was like the harmony of early morning, the whisper of new leaves brushing against the dew, the delicateness of flower blossoms coming to life. The energy of her words spun through him with restless temptation, prying him from his dark thoughts about Louis, the bloodbath he'd left behind, and the carnage that awaited innocents if he could not stop the slide.

In his world, craving a woman this intensely was a very, *very* dangerous thing.

He wanted to race toward her.

He wanted to rip aside the canopy of leaves shielding her from his sight.

He wanted to find her, to claim her, to consume her.

So, instead, he stopped and went completely still. He reached out with his preternatural senses, searching the landscape ahead. The mountain was ominously tall. Turbulent dark clouds coated the sky above him, but it wasn't enough to block her presence. He caught the faint scent of woman, pure and delicate, and his gut clenched in response. But still, he didn't move. Instead, he carefully located the pulsing energy of the sword she was guarding. She was between him and the sword, an obstacle that he had to pass in order to retrieve the weapon.

Testing her, he turned left, circling around behind her. As he moved, she shifted, keeping herself between him and the sword. Could she sense him? Was her awareness of him as intense as his awareness of her?

He looked down at the protective symbols on his arms and saw they were still blazing. As long as they were visible, the *sheva* bond could not affect him. No woman could be his soul mate. He was still safe from that fate...but if that was the case, why was he reacting to her so intensely? He had no time for women. He didn't have the luxury to indulge in seduction. He was never distracted from what he had to do.

So, what the hell was going on with her?

He had no time to play games any longer. He needed that sword, and he needed it now, which meant he had to get past her. He was tempted to call out his spears, but he didn't. Never would there come a day when he approached a woman armed. Ever.

So, instead, he straightened up, fisted his hands, and strode right through the undulating shadows toward her.

His feet were silent on the forest floor, and the leaves moved out of his way as he walked, responding to his silent request for passage, as they always did. Ahead of him, he could see that the trees thinned, and he knew he was approaching a clearing.

His weapons still burning in his arms, responding to the risk she presented, Dante stepped forward through the last of the foliage and into an open, exposed area.

He didn't see her.

Disappointment surged through him as he quickly scanned the vicinity. Trees stood tall above him, their branches long and spindly, tangling into each other, weaving a canopy that protected this area from the rest of the world. Sparse grass clung to barren dirt. Ancient rocks lay battered, half-submerged in the weary ground. He could sense the suffering of this place, of the people who had once lived and died in this clearing. So much to tell him, and yet the one thing he wanted to see was hidden from him. He saw no sign of her, but her presence was strong, a vibrating energy of light and dark. "Show yourself," he commanded.

No response. Not even another whispered reply on the wind.

Awareness still prickling on his neck, he walked further into the clearing, reaching out with his senses, searching for a ripple in the atmosphere that would reveal her location. Out into each direction he sent queries, and then he found her. A block in the transference of energy, a shield of sorts, in the northwest end of the clearing.

He turned toward it, his hands still flexing. Behind her, he could feel the sword's energy calling to him, more intensely than ever before. The urge to respond to its summons was thundering through him, almost impossible to resist, but he refused to acknowledge it. This woman, this mysterious woman who was guarding it, this sensual temptation of danger...she was what he needed to deal with first.

He had learned many lessons from his bastard father, one of which was to never, *ever* underestimate the enemy.

He kept his gaze riveted on the swirl of feminine energy that he'd located. He couldn't see her, but he knew she was there. "I am going to take the sword," he said.

"No." Her voice was clear, its raw intensity like a shot to his gut. It wasn't simply feminine, it was powerful and strong, rich with sensuality. "Walk away."

"It's been calling to me." He took a step closer, and felt a sudden burst of wind slam against his chest, as if she'd shoved the air at him as a warning. Could she manipulate air? He'd never heard of that. "The sword wants me to retrieve it."

"Do not touch it." As the words filled the air, a faint mist began to glisten in the location he was watching, like millions of dew droplets in the first rays of morning light.

Adrenaline and anticipation roared through him, and he was riveted by the rainbow-colored prisms as they glittered and sparkled, becoming less transparent. Then he saw her face beginning to take shape. An incredible, vibrant turquoise began to glow as it slid into the shape of her nose, a delicate slope of pure femininity. Smooth cheeks of perfection, the sensual curve of her jaw, parted lips. Her hair began to appear, tumbling down around her in violet and turquoise cascades of thick curls. And then, her eyes. Dante stood, transfixed, as her eyes appeared, vibrant blue-violet pools flanked with long, thick lashes, watching him intently.

Her body began to manifest. Long, delicate arms, a mystical dress clinging to her body, showing small breasts of surreal temptation, hips that bled into lean legs, bare feet that seemed to fade right into the grassy tufts by her toes.

"What are you?" he asked, his voice gruffer than he'd intended.

"I don't exist here." There was a sudden shimmer, as if a thousand prisms had shifted position, and then she was standing before him, fully corporeal, with flesh as human as his. Her cascade of colors shifted into a rich, decadent shower of brown curls, and an endless temptation of flesh so pale it looked as though it had never seen the sun. But her eyes were the same, a vibrant, iridescent symphony of violet, rich blue, and enchantment.

She was beauty. This was the first moment in his life that he truly understood what the word meant. Not simply her appearance, but her entire aura. It was pulsing and shimmering, rich with sensations that seemed to reach inside him and shatter the darkness that clung to every cell in his body.

Stunned, he limped toward her, compelled by the need

to touch her, to see if she was real. She lifted her chin regally as he neared. She did not retreat, but her muscles tensed, and a ripple of fear echoed through the air.

He stopped a mere foot from her and raised his hand. Gently, almost afraid that he would shatter the mirage, he brushed his fingers ever so lightly over the ends of her curls. Silken strands glided through his fingers, the softest sensation he'd ever experienced. She closed her eyes and went utterly still, as if drinking in his touch with every ounce of her being.

"You *do* exist here," he said softly, forcing himself to drop his hand, trying to shield himself against the depth of his urge to slide his hand down her arm, to feel the warmth of her skin against his. Again, he looked down at his protective markings and saw they were still blazing as black as they had the first time he'd finally succeeded in manifesting them. This wasn't a *sheva* compulsion. It couldn't be. So what was it? He had one goal, one mission, and limited time to do it, and yet he felt like he wanted nothing more than to be in her presence and to touch her. To kiss her. To possess her.

She opened her eyes, and he saw that they had darkened to deeper blue-violet, though they still had the glittery sparkles in them. "You are worthy," she said softly. "I can feel your strength, your capability. The sword has chosen well. Too well," she added, the regret obvious in her voice.

Dante had no idea what the hell was going on, not with the sword that had been summoning him, not with this woman who had manifested from a glittery mist, and not with his burning desire for her. Weapons, he understood. All this? No, but he was going to figure it out, and fast. "My name is Dante Sinclair, Calydon warrior." He did not say he was the unwilling leader of the famous Order of the Blade. He did not add that he was the only one left of his kind. He did not explain that he was the only warrior still alive who could possibly save the earth from rogues, and that he was dying, fast. "Who are you?"

"Dante Sinclair," she repeated, sending warmth spiraling

through him as she said his name. She made it sound poetic, like a great gift offered to the very earth upon which they stood. She gave a low curtsy. "My name is Elisha, daughter of the   Queen of Darkness. Soon to be consort to the master Adrian."

Dante went cold at her words. "Consort?" That one word had chased every other bit of information she'd offered out of his mind. "What does that mean?" Shit. He knew what that meant. But he needed to know what *she* meant by it, by her future.

She rose to her feet, and something flickered in her eyes, something he couldn't decipher, but she definitely had reacted to his fury about her becoming some bastard's consort.

She raised her hand and brushed her fingers over his cheek. "Your anger at my words is beautiful." Her touch was like silk, the whisper of a new dawn across his skin. Without speaking, he laid his hand over hers, pressing her palm to his face. Her hand was cool, her touch drifting through his body like the cleansing rain of a raging summer storm. He'd never felt relief like she was giving him. The world had never paused long enough for him to breathe air so fresh or touch something so soft and pure. He had never seen it. Never felt it. Never even considered it.

All he knew about purity and innocence was from watching it be destroyed by his father and the rest of the Order. And yet, here, this woman...it was like a soothing balm had been laid over his soul, easing the torment of over a hundred years.

Her gaze went to his. "You have freedom here, in the earth realm. I can sense it about you. Your heart—" She laid her other hand on his chest, moving even closer to him. "—it beats differently than mine. I can feel its freedom. It's like the purest magic, born of innocence and honor." A sense of awe appeared on her face, and Dante felt his world begin to close in on him as he tumbled into her spell.

Unbidden, his hand slid to the back of her neck. He needed to touch her. To kiss her. To claim her. To make her his.

Her eyes widened, and she froze, going utterly still. "No," she whispered. "This cannot be."

"Just like how you don't exist in the earth realm?" He bent his head, his lips hovering a breath from hers. He had to kiss her. He had to know she was real. He had to know that something as pure and beautiful as Elisha actually existed... and that he could be a part of it. "Because you *do* exist. And this *can* be, because it's happening right now."

"No!" A gust of wind suddenly slammed into his chest and thrust him backwards. He landed ten feet away, on his ass, a pawn in the grasp of her power.

Damn. That was impressive. A woman who could defend herself against the poison of the Order? Perhaps *she* was the answer he sought, not the sword...but even as he thought it, there was a fresh surge of compulsion from the sword, still relentlessly calling to him.

With a groan that he didn't mean to let slip, he vaulted back to his feet, unsettled that he'd let his need for her dictate his actions. Had he really just considered seducing her when his last hope for saving innocents before he died lay hidden behind her, only a half-day's run from the carnage that Louis had caused? Shit. He was weak, too weak to bear the mark of the leader of the Order.

Cold, steely focus was required to discharge the duties of the Order, not a man so weak that his desperate need for a woman could interfere with his duty. He lowered his head, studying her more carefully. The power of a woman. Not just *a* woman. *This* woman. Never had he been tempted like this before. What the hell was she? A princess? What in the hell was going on? "Who is the Queen of Darkness? And what realm are you from, if you're not from the earth realm?"

Elisha was facing him, her hands dangling loosely by her sides, her gaze blazing. "You must leave," she said urgently.

"You must."

There was no chance of that. "Where is the sword from, Elisha?" He began to walk toward her again, fighting to keep from favoring his bad leg, but this time, it wasn't about seduction. It was about his mission, his job, his calling. "How is it calling me?"

"No." Once again, she sent air at him, pushing him backwards, but this time he was ready.

He simply braced himself and shoved forward, cutting through the invisible wall.

Her face tightened with fear. "Halt!" she commanded, with the imperious force of the royalty she'd claimed to be.

He stopped. "Tell me why." She was soon going to be some man's consort? Really? *Shit.* Why was he thinking about *that* when he was facing down an enemy? He schooled his thoughts away from seduction, desire, and temptation, and faced the princess. "Tell me what's going on."

Dante was far more than she'd even imagined. His dark eyes were intense, staring at her as if he would not hesitate to pry every last bit of information out of her that he wanted. But his hands...she couldn't stop thinking about what it had felt like to have his fingers in her hair. It had been so gentle, so incredibly enticing. He hadn't hurt her, and he hadn't even tried. The man was covered in blood. His clothes were tattered. Deep wounds were already healing in his flesh. His foot was mangled and blackened, contaminated with the terrible dark aura of the nether-realm. His short, dark hair made him look young, but his eyes carried many years of pain and hardship, and his well-muscled body was chiseled with the stress of a physical life.

Although she was no longer touching him, she could still feel the prickle of whiskers beneath her palm. She would never forget the warmth of his skin, or the way his hand had pressed onto hers. She had never experienced anything like it. There had been so much humanity and gentleness in his touch. It had been so beautiful to experience physical contact that hadn't been initiated for a dark purpose, but had occurred simply because it felt good. Was that how it was on earth? Or just with Dante?

As he stared at her, waiting for her answers, a slow sinking feeling of dread formed in the pit of her belly. He would ruin her, if she gave him a chance. He would ruin everything, here and now, and when she returned.

She had to make him understand and get him to leave. Now. Fast. Before he could shift the tide in the wrong direction. "My mother is the Queen of Darkness," she began.

"I know. You said that." Dante looked past her, toward the sword, which was hidden at the bottom of a clear pool. "I'm going to check on the sword while we talk." He strode right toward her, and she stepped aside as he passed, knowing that she had to give him the illusion of his own power. Dante would not yield if pushed. She had to make him understand and choose the right path. Force was only for the last, desperate moment. "Who is the Queen of Darkness?" he asked.

"The queen's darkness is a realm on the far side of the nether-realm," she said, hurrying to catch up as he walked. His gait was uneven, and she suspected his foot was as painful as it appeared.

He looked at her sharply. "The nether-realm is where demons are spawned. Calydons were created from a stream tainted by the nether-realm. It's the underworld. There's nothing past it."

"There is. It's—" She hesitated, having no words to describe the horror of what it was. "It's more than the nether-realm."

Dante paused, looking over at her. His eyes narrowed, and she saw a sudden alertness in them. "What do you mean, 'more?'"

For a moment, the need to explain burned inside her, a desire to show him what life was like for her, to show him the ugliness that lay fermenting inside her, but suddenly, she couldn't bear to do it. She wanted him to keep looking at her as he first had, as if she were the most beautiful thing he'd ever seen, not the tainted ugliness she really was. No one had ever looked at her the way he just had, and she didn't want to let that go. Not yet. "My mother is thousands of years old," she said instead. "She wants more than the queen's realm to rule. She wants the earth."

Dante was facing her now. "And?"

"There's a veil between the queen's realm and the rest of existence. The magical filament was put in place thousands of years ago by the earth's protectors. They could not destroy my mother, but they could contain her. She has spent the last thousand years having this sword crafted, the sword that has been calling you. It's been forged in the shadows of the queen's darkness, fed with the blood of the greatest beasts, and cursed with black magic so powerful that only two beings can harness it."

Dante's eyebrows went up. "And why is it calling me?"

"Because it was sent to this world to find a warrior strong enough to wield it." She met his gaze. "If you touch it, it will own you. You'll be compelled to take it into the mountain and sever the curtain that binds the queen's darkness. Her world will spill into this one, and all hope will be lost." Elisha took a step forward. "You cannot touch it, Dante. If you do, you'll destroy all life."

His face was inscrutable as he studied her, and she had no idea if he believed her. The sword's call was getting stronger. Was he strong enough to resist it? "Dante—"

"I want to see it." Then, before she could stop him, he turned away and sprinted toward the hidden pool, the one that would be visible only to those that the sword had chosen. She raced after him, her feet landing soundlessly on the rough ground as she ran.

Dante reached the pool and went down on one knee, his dark eyes riveted on the surface of the pool. Elisha knelt beside him, following his intense stare. The sword lay at the bottom. It was a smoky black, undulating as if it were alive. The blade was long and curved, with a triple spike on the tip for piercing the veil. The handle was plain, not a jewel to be seen, yet it seemed to dance and sing with a beauty beyond words. Elisha glanced at Dante, unsure what image the sword would reveal to him. "Do you see it?"

"It's dark red," he said quietly. "I can see the drops of blood swirling in it, and the glitter of jewels." He passed his hand over the surface of the water. "It contains so much power. Enough to bring down armies with a single blow. Even rogue Calydons."

Elisha's heart fell at his description. The sword was showing him everything that would tempt a man. Power. Destruction. Wealth. "It will destroy the earth," she said again, her hand sliding to her hip where she'd hidden the dagger in the folds of her dress. After being so close to Dante and breathing in the deeply masculine scent that was his, she didn't want to kill him and deliver him to a death worthy only of the beasts who so willingly carried out her mother's commands. She wanted him to touch her again, to show her that kindness she'd glimpsed a moment ago. She wanted him to ignite in her those swirling desires that felt like wildfire unleashed upon her soul.

Dante turned his head to look at her, and she saw a sheen of sweat across his forehead. Pain? Temptation? His eyes were blazing, and she knew that the sword was calling him fiercely, and that he was fighting with every bit of strength to resist its call. "What would you have me do instead?" he asked.

Hope leapt through her. "Walk away."

He met her gaze. "And then what?"

"Then stay away." Was the man dense? Was it not

obvious?

"No." He turned toward her, until they were only inches apart. "I mean, Elisha, what then? Will it haunt me night and day? Will it ever give up?" He leaned forward, lowering his voice. "Because I'm not a machine, Elisha, and I won't be able to resist it forever. That thing is burning through my flesh right now. I can feel it in my hand. I know exactly how the handle will fit against my palm. I can hear the tones of its energy humming through my head. It's a low, violent rumble that bleeds power. I can see the carnage spread out before it as I raise it above my head. I can see my enemies fall, crumbling beneath its power."

"It's a lie," she said urgently.

"No, it's not. The sword is that powerful, and we both know it." He looked again at the pool. "Do you know who my enemies are, Elisha? They're my own kind. Rogue Calydons who destroy innocents. Women. Children. Good men. No one is strong enough to stop them." Regret and bitterness were heavy in his voice. "No one except me, and I'm dying." He reached out a hand, and she tensed, her heart pounding as he flattened his palm over the surface of the water, not touching it, but so close. "But this sword could do it. It would bring down anyone I wanted. Do you see, Elisha? With this sword, I could bring peace all by myself." His voice faded, and his expression became grim, almost as if he, too, could see the dangerous fate for any who wielded it. "It will corrupt anyone who touches it," he whispered. "It's like my father himself."

"It will bring death," she hissed. "It's a lie!"

Dante dropped his hand suddenly and leapt backward, throwing himself a far distance from the pool. He landed on his back, skidding across the earth before he finally stopped. He sat up, draping his arms over his knees, but he did not rise. Sweat was streaming down his face, rivulets streaking the dried blood and dirt still on his body from the battle he'd been engaged in before he'd come. "It feels so fucking real to me," he said, his eyes blazing. "It will give me the one thing I want."

She leapt to her feet. "It will give my mother what she wants." Instinctively, she pushed air against him, building a wall between him and the pool.

Dante laughed softly, brushing his hand through her protection. "You can't stop me from taking it. That's why the sword picked me. Because I'm stronger than you."

"I will stop you." She pulled the dagger out of her dress and let him see it. "The Blade of Cormoranth," she said.

Dante's gaze went sharply to the blade that she knew he'd heard of. All warriors had. It was legendary. It would kill whatever the person wielding it wanted to destroy. There was no defense against it. None at all.

Dante studied the blade, and he dragged his gaze to her as he stood up, his long, muscular body unfolding so gracefully from his seated pose. "And what if you kill me, Elisha? Won't the sword call another instead?"

"I'll kill him, too."

"And another? And another? And another?" He took a step toward her, and Elisha stiffened. "I know the legend of that blade. The poison in it will eat away at the mind of the person wielding it, until the very person who used it to destroy becomes its worst victim. It will destroy you, and then the sword will be free to claim its new owner, won't it?"

"I don't care." She tightened her grip on the handle of the dagger. "I'll do whatever it takes."

"Instead of killing me," he said, easing to a stop in front of her, "you can believe that I'm as good as the sword thinks I am, and realize that I, and I alone, might have the power to control the sword, instead of it controlling me. I might own it and bend it to *my* will." Even as he said it, more sweat beaded on his brow, and he swayed, as if he were going to fall.

Instinctively, she reached for him, her hand closing on his arm. He went rigid under her touch, his hooded gaze intense on hers. "Do you know how weak we all are? No warrior that I know can resist the corruption that absolute power can give. No one." He looked past her at the sword again. "I cannot allow anyone else to be burdened with it. It is my duty. That is why it called me." He rubbed his finger over a mark on his wrist, his face grim. "It fucking has to be me, doesn't it? I'm the one who has to wield it and be stronger than it. I can't walk away and let someone else deal with it instead."

For a split second, hope leapt through her at his words, at his conviction that he could defeat the sword. But at the same time, she knew it was a false hope. "No one is stronger than that sword."

"No?" Dante looked at her. "My name is Dante Sinclair," he said again, his voice low and dangerous. "My father raped my mother to create me, and then kidnapped me when I was five. When she came after me, he slayed her in front of me, claiming that the right of the Order to create more of their kind trumped all else. I watched all the other Order members do the same. They raped. They kidnapped. They beat their sons to make them tough. And then each of them met their *sheva* and went rogue, desecrating the very earth that they were sworn to protect. I've seen darkness. I've lived hell. And I will not, *will not*, allow that kind of darkness to spawn in my world, and I will *not* allow a sword to turn me into that kind of monster."

His words were so raw with emotion and pain that her heart seemed to freeze in her chest, and tears sprang to her eyes. Dear God, who spoke like that against terrible things? Who lived a life in protest of it? "I don't understand," she whispered, stunned by his words. By all he had suffered. By his hatred of the things she lived with every day of her life. She didn't understand how he could mean what he said, how he could truly live the passion that he'd spoken.

"You don't understand?" Dante limped forward, sliding his hand behind her neck, as if to force her to understand. "I'm all that's left," he said. "I'm it. I'm the last hope that the innocents of this earth have to protect themselves from those who used to be my friends, my brothers, and my teammates. I am all that stands between them and their demise. I won't abandon them, no matter what. A sword bewitched by a queen of darkness means nothing to me. It cannot ensnare me, not at the cost of the innocents I swore to protect. Nothing, *nothing*, can deflect me from my purpose. I will protect them!" He suddenly strode past her, plunged his fist into the water, and grabbed the sword.

CHAPTER FOUR

Elisha screamed in protest as Dante touched the sword, but it was too late. An explosion of colors filled the clearing, sending sparks of blue, turquoise, orange, red, yellow, and green cascading through the air, shooting into the night sky, falling in colorful remnants to the parched earth. The air filled with the screams and whistles of a thousand armies, saluting their greatest master.

Dante raised the sword above his head, pointing it to the heavens as smoke poured from the end of the blade, great billows of darkness so intense that the clearing was instantly consumed. It became as dark as the blackest night, until the only light that remained were the fading sparks fighting for a last breath. He raised his face, and smoke poured down his arms, coating his flesh with black soot, owning his body, his soul, and his mind.

For a moment, Elisha stood transfixed, stunned by the sheer power flooding the area, and by the way Dante's already muscular body seemed to swell with vile, tainted strength. Dismay filled her chest as a bellow erupted from the depths of his soul, the battle cry of victory, of a man who had secured his greatest desire. For a moment there, during his speech, she'd felt the intensity of his conviction, and she'd believed that maybe, just maybe, he was the man who could end all this...

Yet there he was, a statue being consumed by the sword that was so much more powerful for an earth-bound male—

"Wind! Give me wind!" Dante's voice ripped through her mind, a command so fierce that it shattered the hold that the moment had on her.

She responded instantly, throwing out her hands and blasting him with such force that his skin rippled and the trees behind him flattened. With a howl of outrage, Dante spun around and swung the sword, hurling it at the very trees she'd leveled. It flew from his hands, streaking through the air like an enchanted stream of black magic, and slamming hilt-deep into the roots of the nearest tree. The tip was jammed so deeply in the trunk, it was as if it were trying to sever the tree's soul from its physical form.

Disbelieving shock froze her. He'd managed to release the sword!

The moment Dante let go of the sword, the night screamed in fury, the smoke vanished, and the colors faded. He dropped to his hands and knees, his head bowed, his body shaking violently, his torso heaving as fierce breaths fought in his chest.

Elisha raced over to him, stunned by what had just happened. "You let go of it. You broke its hold on you." She couldn't believe it. She'd never seen anything like that happen before. Ever.

Slowly, Dante raised his head to look at her. His eyes were streaked with red, and there was blood trickling from the corner of his mouth. "I must confess," he said grimly, "that was a hell of a lot more difficult than I thought it was going to be."

She almost smiled at the enormity of his understatement. "Did you think I was lying about the power of the sword?"

"No. I just thought you didn't realize what a hero I am." With a groan, Dante collapsed, and then rolled onto his back, his chest still heaving. "Turns out, the queen of darkness makes a better sword than I gave her credit for. Or, conversely, it turns out that I'm weaker than I imagined."

"You're not weak, Dante. For you to be able to release that sword after it had claimed you is incredible. You're powerful beyond words." Elisha sank down beside him, her body shaking with relief. How could he sound normal after that? "How did you release it?"

"I don't know." He draped one arm across his forehead. His flesh was burned and swirling with the power of the sword that was still inside him. "It all happened so fast I wasn't ready for it." He glanced at her. "The wind helped."

She smiled. "Better than the Blade of Cormoranth." Then her smile faded. "So, you'll walk away now?" Even as she asked the words, regret filled her. She didn't want him to depart. Not this powerful, incredible man who spoke of protecting innocents with such passion that she'd felt it in her own heart. Not this man who had somehow, incredibly, been able to break the sword's hold on him. Not this man, whose mere nearness seemed to pulse deep inside her, to call her, to beckon to her. "You must walk away," she added, forcing herself to say the words she had to say. "You must understand now how dangerous it is."

Dante let out his breath. "I saw the destruction that it carries. I felt it. The sword is..." He looked at her. "It's the worst suffering, the worst hell, the most brutal death that could ever be conceived of, a thousand times over, for an eternity. It's ruthless destruction, at all cost, with no conscience or humanity. It's worse than the Order."

She nodded, surprised that he had been able to grasp the depths of the darkness that lived within the sword. "That's my world."

"Well," Dante said quietly, "I can't let it be this world. It can't be turned loose." He met her gaze. "No man can resist that."

"No. I don't know how you did."

"You did it."

She looked sharply at him. "What?"

"You did it. You kept the corruption at bay." A faint smile touched his face, and he brushed his hand over the ends of her hair. "I kept hearing your voice," he said softly, haltingly, as if he were articulating a truth even he didn't quite grasp. "Through all the noise the sword was making, I kept hearing your voice, telling me to come back to you."

She frowned, her heart pounding at the intimacy of his touch. "I didn't say that."

"You did. I heard you." He met her gaze. "It was you," he said quietly. "You were the purity and innocence I held onto to keep the darkness of the sword from taking me. Your wind helped me." He brushed his finger over her lips. "The wind you create is like the kiss of your soul, and it freed me."

Warmth began to spiral through her, like the hot kiss of desire. "I didn't do anything—"

"You did." He sat up then, with an ease she hadn't expected, until she saw that his skin was already almost fully healed, that his body was recovering with surreal speed... except for his foot, which seemed even more deformed than it had been when he'd arrived such a short time ago. What had happened to him?

He reached for her, but she pulled back, scrambling out of his range as she leapt to her feet.

Dante stood at the same time, catching her arm before she could get out of his reach. She froze, unable to force herself to resist as he slowly, ever so slowly, drew her back toward him. "Every Calydon warrior has a *sheva*," he said in a low, rough voice as his fingers slid up her arm. "The soul mate that he must bond with, but once they complete all five stages of the bond, destiny commands he will go rogue and destroy everything that matters to them both. The only way to stop him is for his *sheva* to kill him, and then herself. It is the way. It is the fate that has befallen every single member of the Order, except me. I am the last one standing, the last one who has not been destroyed by our destiny. The *sheva* destiny is unstoppable, an obsession that twists, destroys, and kills."

She caught her breath as he pulled her against him, so their bodies were touching hip to chest. "I can't be a *sheva*," she said. "I'm not of this world. I can't be bound."

"I doubt that would stop it, but I have taken precautions anyway," he said, locking one arm behind her lower back. "I spent months training until I could manifest the ancient protections to keep the *sheva* bond from being able to grip me. If you were my *sheva*, we could do every bonding stage a thousand times over, and it would do nothing." His eyes were glittering, so dark and intense that she felt as though he could see right into her soul, as if he knew all the darkness the queen had cursed her with.

Fierce, unfamiliar longing seared through her, a need unlike anything she'd ever experienced, the same desire that he'd awoken in her since the first moment she'd sensed him. It was too dangerous, too strange, and too risky. "Let me go," she whispered.

He didn't soften his grip. Instead, he raised his free hand, sliding it through her hair in a touch so tantalizing that her belly started to tremble. "Since you cannot be my *sheva*," he said, "I don't need to fear the intensity of my response to you. I don't need to fear how badly my very soul burns to make you mine. I'm not arrogant enough to think that I'm unstoppable, and I'm wise enough to understand when I have been given the gift of strength I do not have on my own, the ability to be a better man than I truly am...which is what you do for me."

"No." She swallowed, her heart thundering in her ears at the words that were so beautiful, that seemed to mirror exactly the way she was responding to him. "I *do* need to fear this connection between us," she said. "I can't be distracted from my purpose. I have to be able to kill you, not fantasize about your kisses and—"

"We have a common purpose." He bent his head, trailing

his lips ever so softly down her neck, sending ripples of intense desire through her. "My only mission is to protect this world and to secure its safety before I die. Your goal is to stop that sword from being used to sever the veil and destroy the earth." He pulled back to look at her, his eyes blazing with intensity. "There is only one way to make that happen. I will destroy the sword so that no one can ever use it, and you will give me the strength to resist it. I do not fear you, Elisha. I embrace you."

She shook her head, trying to keep her mind focused on what mattered, not on the feel of his body against hers. "No, no, no, that will never work. The only way to destroy the sword is to return it to its source. To do that, you have to sever the veil and plunge it into the inferno of darkness at the base of the veil. That will shut the veil again, but during the time it's open, so much can escape, and the power of the sword is so strong that it will consume you the moment you use it for its intended purpose. Even you will not be able to withstand its force once you use it to sever the veil. There's no way—"

"There is always a way," he said, tightening his grip on the back of her hair. "You're my power, Elisha. You're my key. I don't know how, and I don't know why, but a warrior who ignores his greatest asset is a fool, and I am not a fool." He gripped her tightly. "I must stop the slaughter. *I must.*"

A part of her, a deep wrenching part of her, cried at his words, at the certainty on his face that she was his salvation. "I'm the princess of darkness, Dante. I'm not your salvation. I can't be. I'm your death. I'm your suffering. I'm your—"

He cut her off with a kiss of such relentless intensity that all the arguments, all her determination, all her certainty shattered into heart wrenching fragments, leaving her with nothing more than a raw, aching need for more. She craved the gentle, evocative caress of his hands, the decadent taste of his lips, and the deep sound of his voice. He made her yearn for all the beautiful things that she'd never been allowed to experience, that she'd never even known could be real.

It was almost overwhelming to be in his arms. His kiss was too tempting for her to resist. His embrace was too beautiful for her to rise above. All she wanted was to fall into the magic of his seduction and to lose herself in the sheer strength of his body and the honor of his soul. But she didn't even know how to respond to it or how to accept it. She had no clue how to breathe it into her spirit to hold it close forever. She had no experience with kindness, with gentleness, or with the indescribable desire that ensnared her in its grasp with its merciless temptation.

As he deepened the kiss, Dante gently ran his hands down her arms, encircled her wrists, and then drew them around his neck. Surprised delight danced through her at the movement, and she slid her fingers into his hair, marveling at the softness of the strands. His hands were a wondrous seduction as they slid back down her hips, pulling her more tightly against his hardened cock. With a low growl, he angled his head, kissing her more deeply and ruthlessly, as if a rising urgency was driving him now.

His kisses were no longer controlled and precise. They were ragged and desperate, exactly how she felt. God, she needed more of him, so much more. She barely even understood the need driving her or the pressure building inside her. All she knew was that each touch, each kiss, and each caress that he offered stoked the fire more.

His hand gripped the flimsy material of her dress, and with one swift move, he tugged it up, baring her leg. He slid his palm over her thigh and lifted her leg onto his, easing his fingertips along her flesh, like the white-hot brands of fire that steamed so high over the valleys in her homeland.

She craved his touch with a fierceness she could barely comprehend. Never had she wanted to be kissed. Never had a man's touch made her soul ache for more. Never had she grasped the seduction of touch, of kisses, of the scent of a man, or of the feel of taut muscles beneath her palms. Never, until now, until Dante's body was against hers, until she could taste him in her mouth, until she had fallen under the power of his spell.

"Elisha," he whispered, breaking the kiss to trail his mouth down her neck, a decadent temptation that made her shiver.

She gripped his shoulders, holding on as tightly as she could, terrified that the moment would end, that somehow, he would slip out of her grasp and she'd be flung back into her world and the life she faced every day—

"It's moving." Dante broke the kiss suddenly, staring past her. "It's actually moving."

She whirled around to see the sword undulating in the trunk of the tree as if it were trying to free itself. Dante looked down at his open hand and flexed it. There were imprints on his palm in the shape of the sword's hilt, as if he were already holding it. "It's strong," he muttered. "Jesus, it's strong."

Elisha's heart sank, and a sense of cold desolation chased away the warmth and beauty of his kisses as their reality returned. "The connection between you both was forged when you held it in your grasp. You can't break it now. It won't let you go." She stared at him. "You can't escape it, Dante. It's too late."

Dante looked at her, and a broad grin broke out on his face. "Well, then, I guess you're just going to have to go with my plan, aren't you? Let me take the sword, sever the veil, and then destroy the sword."

She blinked. "No, I must kill you. I told you—"

"No." Dante's smile vanished so quickly that it was almost scary. He grasped her arm and pulled her close, his eyes blazing. "You might not be my *sheva*, Elisha, but you burn in my veins as if you were the fire that sustains me. I don't have to fight it, because there's no *sheva* destiny. My life is hell. It's darkness. It's death. Every day, I watch people die. People I care about, people who counted on me, people who once saved my life, I watch them all die. They fall to my blade or someone else's. I hear the screams of the people I was supposed to save. Every minute of the day, I hear the roars of the warriors I couldn't guide to salvation. Every time I close my eyes, I see them in the throes of death, by my hand. Every single breath I take, I feel the agony of those who died because I failed them, because the Order I was born to lead betrayed them."

His pain attacked her like a great beast, clawing at her heart. "Dante, I'm so sorry—"

"I'm not." His grip on her tightened. "Because those nightmares keep me going. They make me fight harder to find a way to turn this tide. I drink in their pain because that's what keeps me protected from failing. I should have died from this poison long ago, but I could not allow it until I had finished my mission." He held up his arm, showing her the markings on his flesh, the ancient runes of protection. "That's why I was able to manifest these. I used the pain to make myself stronger than my destiny."

Tears filled her eyes for the suffering that he lived by. It was the same as the suffering she saw every day, but in her world, it was celebrated as a beautiful thing, as a statement of all that was right in the world. She alone had shed tears for those who had died, and yet here was a man, this powerful, beautiful man, who felt the same sorrow she did. She took his arm and pressed her lips to the markings, knowing no other way to show him her respect and admiration, and to share with him how deeply she understood his suffering.

His eyes glittered as he took her hand, guiding it to his lips, where he pressed a kiss against the flat of her palm. "I embrace the pain," he said, "but you are like this great gift of light cutting through the darkness. The memories and the suffering make me strong, but you, Elisha, you touch something inside me that makes me the man that I have never been able to be." His dark eyes met hers. "You complete the circle. I don't know how," he whispered, almost absently. "It makes no sense that you awaken emotions in me, and that those emotions make me stronger...but that's what's happening."

Warmth flooded her, a beauty so bright she felt like it would blind her...and she knew it would do exactly that, blinding her to what she had to do. "No, no," she said, pulling her hand free. "Don't say that. It doesn't matter what's between us. I must stop you—"

"No." He put his hand over hers as she reached for the dagger. "Don't you understand what I'm saying, Elisha? When a Calydon meets his *sheva*, he is consumed by an instinct so primal, so complete, that he will do *anything* to keep her safe. He could not harm her. He would not harm her. And he would never, ever allow harm to befall her."

Her heart pounded at his words, but she shook her head, fighting not to fall into the magic of what he spoke. "I'm not your *sheva*, and I'm not in danger," she said. "You're the one in danger, because I have to kill you—"

"I can't let you use that blade," he said, encircling her wrist with a touch so delicate that she knew it was a lie. He would never let her pull away if she tried, despite his feather-light touch. "It will destroy you, and I, as the man who you have claimed, cannot allow that harm to befall you."

She stared at him as his words sank in. "I haven't claimed you—"

"You have. And I—" he continued, as if she hadn't spoken. "—claim you. Right here. Right now. As the woman who will guide me to the mission I was meant to lead."

Then he kissed her. Not just a kiss. A *claiming*.

Fear tore through her, terror of being trapped by a man to do his bidding, of being thrust into the future she'd been fighting to evade. But as his lips touched hers, there was also something else, something other than fear.

Peace. Desire. Lust. Need.

They were all the wrong things to feel. They were the emotions that made her too vulnerable. They were the temptations that would destroy her. She knew she had to break the connection, but even as she thought it, the light in her soul that had been dark for so long suddenly flared to life, awakened by his kiss, by his embrace, by all that he was.

Chapter Five

Dante could feel the sword summoning him.

He could hear the hum of its magic blistering in his head.

He could barely resist the burning of his palms as they craved the sword they had once touched.

But even stronger, even more powerful, even more compelling, was the taste of Elisha's lips, the feel of her smooth flesh, and the incredible strength of her spirit. She was courage. She was bravery. And she was *passion*.

With a low growl, he swept his arm around her lower back, lifting her against him as he kissed her, burying himself in her presence. With each kiss, with each mingled breath, with each pulse of desire, the pull of the sword lessened, subjugated to his need for her. He didn't understand how she was making him stronger. Passion led to corruption. Emotions led to betrayal. The only path to being the great protector was to be so cold, so focused, that *nothing* could tempt him aside. And yet, the opposite was happening with Elisha.

Her kisses were innocence layered with raw desire, a combination that ignited in him the need to both protect her and to awaken her sensuality pulsing tentatively just beneath the surface. "Elisha," he whispered. "Give yourself over to me. Let us combine our power and rise together."

She made a small noise of protest, and he caught it with another kiss as he ran his hand along her thigh, pulling her leg higher on his hip. Her belly was against his erection, the soft flesh of her stomach trembling. Fire seemed to sear his veins, a need unlike anything he'd ever felt before. It was as if she was his breath, the beating of his heart, and the source of his blood. His life was in her hands. His future was entangled in her kisses. His hope for all he sought lay in the heart that beat within her delicate frame.

He didn't understand how this could be happening between them. He was a man who had spent a lifetime perfecting his shields against the need for a woman, for his *sheva*. He was a warrior who'd strived to erect the steel facade that had failed all the other Order members. He did not believe in passion, warmth, or any emotion that could weaken him. And yet, something about Elisha had broken through all those protections, stripped him raw, and empowered him beyond comprehension.

With one swift move, he swept her up in his arms, cradling her against his chest as he carried her away from the sword to the far side of the clearing, where the only grass remained. As he set her down, easing on top of her carefully, so as not to crush her, he felt her hands go to his chest.

Not to push him away.

To touch him. To explore him. To connect.

He went still, closing his eyes, barely able to restrain himself as her fingers moved across his bare flesh. Her touch was feather-light, so gentle it felt as if she'd never touched a man before. The thought of another man with her made something shift inside him, something dark. His mind flashed back to the comment she'd made when they'd first met about becoming another man's consort. He pulled back, and she jerked her hand away from him, heat flooding her cheeks. "Sorry," she said. "I didn't intend—"

"It's okay." He put her hand back on his chest, fighting

to keep his voice calm. "What did you mean when you said you're going to be another man's consort?"

A delicate furrow appeared between her eyebrows. "Yes. Adrian, one of the masters. My union with him will help secure my mother's power. She needs Adrian on her side."

Dark, ugly anger began to ferment inside him. "And you're willing to do it?"

She blinked. "It doesn't matter if I'm willing. There is no freedom in the queen's realm. I—" She swallowed, and he saw a surge of determination in her eyes. "I do what I must, but there are limits even for me. I couldn't let her destroy the earth."

He didn't understand. The earth was more important than her own body? "Why do you need to protect the earth? You don't even live here."

"I know." A softness filled her eyes, a misty haze as if she were looking past him into memories only she could see. "When I was little, one of the water faeries from the nether-realm slipped through into the queen's darkness. She told me stories of the earth, and she brought me a flower. I couldn't believe how lovely it smelled. Have you ever smelled a flower?"

He scowled. "What?" Smell a flower? Who had time to sniff a plant?

"Everything about the earth sounded so beautiful. After she described it, I dreamed of it always. It was like an oasis in my life, the knowledge that something so beautiful existed even when all I could see was darkness." She smiled and traced a finger along his jaw. "Like you," she said. "Your soul is so full of honor. I've never met anyone like you. I've never known a man with honor. That's why I came here. I couldn't let this world be destroyed, not if I could stop it."

Dante's heart softened at the awe in her eyes. He'd never looked at his world the way she did, but he felt like he could listen for hours to her spin magic about the world that had carried so much grief and death for him. "You've never been here before?"

"No, not until I came with the sword. I can't come here on my own." She smiled again, tracing one finger over his eyebrows and down his nose, as if fascinated by his skin. "The faerie helped me figure out how to merge with the sword so that I could travel with it." She laughed softly, a laugh that was like the magic of fireflies dancing on an August night. "It's ironic, isn't it? The sword that represents such destruction is the blessing that allowed me to come here. I'm connected to it now," she said softly. "Its fate is mine."

Something in her words caught his attention, and Dante narrowed his eyes. "The sword's fate is yours?"

She cleared her throat. "Yes."

"So...if I destroy it..."

She met his gaze. "Yes. If you destroy it, I die as well."

"Then we can't do it." Dante pulled back from her, cutting off their connection with cruel finality.

Elisha sat up, hugging her arms around her, but not able to recreate the warmth he'd generated. "Do what?"

"Destroy the sword." He looked at her. "You can't die."

His statement was so matter-of-fact, so absolute, that she smiled. She barely knew this man, and yet his commitment to her well-being was unshakeable. It was silly, really, that he was reacting that way, but at the same time, it was so beautiful, a gift she'd never had before. "Dante—"

"No." He stood up, his hands balled in fists by his sides. "Absolutely not. There has to be another way. How else can the sword's power be stopped?"

"There's no other way." Elisha watched him pace the clearing. His body was so muscular, so strong, so lethal, but there were also was purity and honesty in his movements. Dante did not hide who he was. He did not skulk in the shadows, ready to strike unsuspecting prey. He stood tall, proud of who he was and what he planned to do. He was everything she'd imagined existed in the earth realm. More than she'd imagined. She simply hadn't understood how good a soul could be until she'd experienced his.

"There has to be." He turned toward her, his eyes blazing. "That sword cannot be allowed to sever the veil. It has to be destroyed without sacrificing you. I don't sacrifice innocents. That's the way it is."

His commitment was beautiful, but it made her sad, because she couldn't allow him to honor it. "Dante," she said quietly. "Sometimes there isn't a way to have it all. The earth must be protected. If it requires my sacrifice, so be it."

"No! That's not acceptable!"

"It is!" She stood up, her own energy roiling. She was so tired of having others tell her what she was allowed to do. She was free now, free to make the choices she wanted. It was time for her to make the difference that she'd never been able to make. "I would rather die to save the earth, than go back into that hell and live the future that is mine. You asked about me being a consort? It's far more than that. It's not just sex I'll give him. It's all of me. My soul. My spirit. My sanity. I'll become a conduit for the power between him and my mother. My father was from the earth realm. My mother used him to create a half-breed child who she could use to reach the earth realm. She killed him as soon as she was pregnant, and she's been using my blood to feed her beasts, to allow them to cross the border and survive in the earth realm."

Dante stared at her. "You're the reason that the dark creatures walk the earth?"

"Yes, they are here because of me. If I die, she loses my blood. She loses me as a tool. Why would I want to preserve my own life at the cost of this world, when all I am is a vessel for her power and depravity?" She spread her hands to encompass the world around them, including Dante. "There's no way, Dante. Just as I was willing to use the Blade of Cormoranth,

I'm willing to sacrifice my life."

"What the hell are you talking about? Just don't go back. You can't kill yourself just because your mother is a psychotic, evil—"

"I have to go back. Although I am partially of the earth realm, my connection to the queen's darkness is what commands me." She walked toward him, her voice urgent with the need to make him understand. "She owns half of me, and she can pull me back. I can resist for a while, but eventually, she will win. The sword is all that is holding me here now, but once that is no longer here, she will be able to reclaim me."

"No!" He grabbed her wrist and yanked her against him so their bodies crashed together. "So we don't destroy the sword. We use it to keep you here."

She gave him a long-suffering look. "Really? So, we do that, and then let the earth die? Is that the plan?"

He narrowed his eyes. "Fuck that. I'll save everyone."

"You can't, and you know that." She looked into his eyes, searching for a truth she needed to know. "The question isn't whether I'm willing to die, or whether you'll let me. The question is whether you're a good enough warrior to destroy the sword once it has severed the veil, or are you not strong enough to resist the lure? Because if you're not, if you sever that veil and can't destroy it, *everything* is done. Everything that matters to you, and to me."

He met her gaze. "If I sever the veil and don't destroy the sword, do you die?"

"No. I return to my world with the sword, and then the queen's darkness enters the earth realm."

He closed his eyes, and his grip tightened on her wrist. "There has to be a third option."

"Walk away from the sword."

"And let someone else try to solve this situation? Fuck that. I've seen other men try to be the hero, and fail. Again and again, they failed. Warriors selected because they alone were strong enough to resist the call of a *sheva*, to rise above the dangers of going rogue, to be cold enough to slaughter the men who were once friends in order to save the innocents. Those men, the ones who were supposed to be the strongest warriors, are all *gone*. I had to kill them. There's no one else besides me. I'm it. And I cannot fail."

As she stared into those blazing eyes, her heart sank. All the weight of the world on one man's shoulders? It was too much for a single soul to bear. How could it not break him? "I'm sorry they all died," she said softly as he turned away, striding across the clearing as if to put distance between them. "I know how it feels." And she did. She lived the deaths of those few people she believed in every day. "There is so little to believe in, that when you lose even that, there's nothing left."

"No," Dante said, turning back toward her. "There's always something left. There's always another chance. There must *always* be redemption." He walked toward her, his body lean and lithe, his muscles rippling like a wild animal stalking his prey.

She tensed and held up her hand to ward him off. "Too much hope breaks you," she replied, unable to keep the ache out of her own heart. "If you believe too much, the crash is too hard—"

"Then you never allow failure." Dante pulled her close, burying his face in her neck as he spoke. She was astounded that his words could be spoken by a man who had already admitted that everyone he believed in had failed, and that all he had tried had come up short. How was he able to say those words, when the earth around him was littered with all he'd lost?

"How can you believe?" she asked, even as she raised her hand to the curve of his neck, needing to touch him, to feel the strength that this warrior bled so fiercely. "I don't understand how you can see success and victory, when there is nothing around but carnage and loss."

"Because there is no other choice." He pressed his face deeper into the crook of her shoulder, his whiskers prickling her. His breath was hot and fiery on her skin, a temptation laced with danger and anger. "There has to be a way," he said. "There *has* to be." He ran his hand down her arm, his touch so soft it was like the whisper of a butterfly's wings. "Such beauty," he said, pressing a kiss to her shoulder. "Such innocence." Another kiss on her collarbone. "Such courage." He feathered a kiss across her cheek. "And so much loss," he said, his voice rough as he whispered his last comment. "You make me want to be the man I have not yet been able to be."

Tears seemed to bleed from her heart, filling her lungs, making her chest ache. She lifted her head to gaze at him. "How can you see me like that, Dante? Don't you know where I'm from? Can't you feel the blackness of the blood that runs through me?" She spread her hands, as if she could see through her flesh. "I am my mother's daughter," she said, raising her gaze to his. "You must see this. You must know the life I've led. Why do you fight what must be done? Sever the veil. Destroy the sword. Let me die before I can do more harm. It's not that complicated."

Dante raised her hand and pressed his lips to her palm. "I see your darkness, but I'm no better," he said softly. "Do you see the blood on my own hands? Do you feel the deaths streaming from my flesh? Do you hear the cries of men as I took their lives, merely because they made the mistake of falling in love? Do you see all that I did when I was too weak to resist my father, before I became strong enough to escape his rule? Do you see all that I have destroyed in the name of protecting innocents?" His voice was heavy and thick, not the determined rant of a warrior. "And do you see all the women, the children, the innocent, who have been cleaved to death by the men I didn't stop in time? Can you see that? I bathe in blood every day of my life. I sleep in death. I walk in murder."

His pain seemed to bleed right into her, his anguish

tearing at her own heart. It was as if she were a part of him, breathing in the very horrors that he lived. She didn't know how she could be feeling him, living him, channeling him, but she was. She recognized the terrible things he'd done, because she had done the same, only she had not done it to protect the innocents. She had done it because it was her legacy. Only if she could save the earth, could she live in peace, knowing that she had done *something* to stop it all.

"And if you die, if I can't do this right and save the woman sent to heal my soul—" That same fire she was beginning to recognize flared in his eyes. "Then, and only then, will I have failed."

Tears brimming in her eyes, she set her hand on his jaw, wanting to touch him, to take away the guilt bleeding from him. "I'm not afraid to do what must be done, Dante. I'm a stranger to you. It shouldn't matter to you. *I* shouldn't matter to you." But even as she said the words, she knew she was lying to herself. There was no way she could wield the Blade of Cormoranth against him. Was it his honor? Was it his bravery? Was it the depth of his commitment to protecting her? She didn't know why her very soul responded to him, why she felt like she could breathe more easily when she was in his arms, but there was no way to deny it.

From the look of fierce denial on his face, she knew he felt the same way...and a fear settled itself in her belly. "If you can't sacrifice me to save the earth, I can't let you have the sword." How would she stop him? How would she make it happen? But even as the questions rattled through her mind, they made her realize the danger that had arisen. Dante's need to protect her would be his doom. He would not be able to destroy the sword and watch her die. And her need to keep him safe would keep her from using the Blade of Cormoranth to stop him.

Dear God, what had they done?

With an agonizing effort, she wrenched herself out of

his arms, desperate to put distance between them. "Don't you see? This connection that's happening between us will make us fail. I can't do what I need to do, and you won't be able to do what you must." He moved toward her, and she shoved air at him fiercely, making him stumble back. "This *sheva* thing you say you are immune to...isn't that the direction we're heading? That we will destroy what matters most? That—"

Dante lunged forward, shattering the wall she'd erected between them. She yelped as he grabbed her, hauling her against him with a fierce roar. "No," he snapped. "It's too late, Elisha. You can't shut me out. I need what we have. I need you—"

"No! I won't destroy the earth, and I won't let you—"

He cut her off with a kiss. No, it was more than a kiss. It was a possession of her soul. An assault of such emotional intensity that it shattered her self-control, her independence, and her commitment to doing what she had to do.

Lost in Dante's gripping embrace and consumed by his kiss, she fell into the respite that he offered, into the humanity, truth, and honor that he shared with her. She became the woman she'd never believed she could be, and she became his.

Dante was not blind to the wisdom of Elisha's words. He knew the risk she presented. He understood that his need to keep her alive was risky, every bit as dangerous as the *shevas* who had brought down the Order one by one. But at the same time, she gave him hope. She gave him purpose. She gave him *life*.

He needed her on levels he couldn't even explain. Her kiss. Her lips. Her laughter. The poignancy of her connection to the earth he traveled. It was all more than he could resist. She was the light that had been fading from his soul with each death, with each failure, with each moment that the Order shriveled and died, falling from their duty and the promise that they'd been founded upon.

He deepened the kiss, pulling her against him, spanning his hand across her lower back. Her spine seemed to melt into the fullness of her hips, and he slid his hands lower, cupping the warm mounds of temptation as he lifted her against him, never lessening his assault on her senses.

She let out a small moan and wrapped her legs around his hips, the small move almost staggering him in its invitation, in its intimacy. "Elisha," he whispered, as he dropped to his knees, locking her on his lap as he grasped her delicate calf, sliding his hand ever-so-slowly along her leg, rising higher and higher, devouring her mouth with kisses so desperate he couldn't get enough.

His cock rose hard and fast, pressing against the junction of her thighs. The fabric between them was too restricting and too thick. He shifted her, sliding both hands under her dress and sliding it upward over her hips, until the delicate material rippled in iridescent waves around her torso. Her skin was hot and soft to his touch, so smooth it felt almost surreal, and yet it was damp with faint perspiration from the heat of their kiss.

Lust burned through him, but it was more than lust. It was a driving, uncontrollable need for her. He wanted to claim her and make her his. He was consumed by the urge to seal their bond until nothing could ever break it. With a low growl, he shifted her off him and unfastened his pants. In one swift move, he had them off. He tossed them on the ground beneath her as a covering. He took her in his arms and kissed her, but this time, he savored it. It was as if his urgency had been sated, knowing that it was close, knowing that he was going to do this, that she was going to be his.

With tantalizing slowness, he eased her dress over her head, her violet-blue eyes locked on his as she raised her arms over her head and allowed him to slip it off her in shimmering cascades of magic and light. He slipped off her silken undergarment, and then froze in shock at the sight of her body...luminescent perfection marred by slashes across her belly, deep scars that had burned themselves into angry black cuts across her flesh.

The anger that rose within him was like a sharp flash of white-hot fury, and he went down on his knees, wrapping his arms around her waist and pressing his lips to each wound. "Who did this?" he asked.

She didn't answer. Instead, she wrapped her arms around his head, holding him to her as he kissed each injury. He could taste the taint in the wounds, the dark energy swirling through them. They were more than pain. They were suffering. They were agony. They were punishment. They were betrayal. He felt her pain in each kiss, her belly trembling in response. Swearing, he eased her back onto the ground, never lifting his head, sending his Calydon healing energy into each kiss, even though he knew it was impossible to share it with anyone except another Calydon or his mate. But still he offered it, thrust it out into her body, willing her soul to accept it.

Heat began to burn, and he placed his hand over her belly, shocked to discover that the warmth was coming from her injuries. It was a pure heat, a healing energy. Had he done that? Had he reached her? Deep satisfaction thrummed through him, and for the first time in his life, he began to understand the allure of a *sheva*. He finally began to comprehend the need to bond with a woman and offer her the kind of protection that only a soul mate could give. Suddenly, the urge to make her his reverberated through him, and the protective runes on his arms seared his flesh, as if his soul was fighting the constraints that he himself had put there so indelibly.

"Come," Elisha whispered, tugging at his shoulders. "Kiss me, Dante. I need to feel your kiss."

He responded to her plea willingly, bracing himself above her as he kissed her. What had been a savoring temptation quickly became a dark, pulsating need for more. A quiet seduction wasn't enough. A kiss would never satisfy what was building between them. His kisses grew deeper, more demanding, more ruthless, and so did hers. He let his hips lower and groaned as he felt the heat of her skin against his. Her nipples were taut against his chest. Her belly was soft beneath his cock. Her hips undulated in an invitation that every cell in his body screamed to accept.

He slid his knee between her thighs, sliding his hand to grasp her calf. He bent his head to her breast, grazing his teeth over her nipple as he raised her leg and wrapped it behind his lower back. She gasped, gripping his shoulders as she writhed beneath him, her back arching in a desperate invitation for more.

Finesse deserted him. Class was no more. Seduction was hopeless. The need to possess her was too great, too deafening, too desperate. It was more than lust. It was a towering inferno of such need that it crawled through every pore of his body, driving him with relentless ferocity. He grabbed her other leg and wrapped it around him, his control shuddering when she hooked her ankles behind his back, relinquishing all her defenses, turning herself over to him completely.

He grasped her hands and pinned them above her head as he moved over her, searching her face, needing to see those violet-blue pools fastening on him, only him. Her thick eyelashes framed her hooded gaze as she watched him intently, as if she needed to see him as much as he needed to see her. "My Elisha," he whispered as he moved his hips until he was pressing against her entrance. "Mine."

She shook her head, twisting restlessly beneath him, her breath coming in shallow gasps. "No one owns me," she said. "No one. No matter what binds me. No matter what shackles hold me. No matter what I am compelled to do. I am the only one who holds my heart."

With those powerful, brave words, Dante felt his world shatter. The anguish and courage in her eyes touched his very heart. He kissed her fiercely, then pressed his lips to her ear.

"Then I shall not seek to own you," he whispered. "But I give all of myself to you. I am yours. Forever." Then with one swift thrust, he buried himself inside her.

She gasped, her belly contracting at the invasion.

He pulled back, meeting her gaze as he began to move inside her. Slowly, ever so slowly, he withdrew, and then drove again, never breaking eye contact with her. The vulnerability in her eyes was agonizing, but at the same time, the trust shining in them made him want to go down on his knees before her and proclaim his loyalty to her.

Suddenly, watching her wasn't enough. He needed to taste her, to touch her, to connect them on all levels. He bent his head and kissed her again, driving deeply, his whole body shaking with the depth of his need for her. Never had he felt like this. Never had he wanted a woman so badly. Never had he understood what it might be like to fall to the *sheva* bond, or to even want to. But in this moment, with Elisha in his arms, he simply wanted the world to stop and hold this moment suspended in eternity.

Despite what she said, Elisha was his. *His.*

CHAPTER SIX

Having Dante inside her was incredible beyond words. His strength, his power, and the way he looked at her seemed to melt the walls around her heart. Elisha felt tears building inside as she watched the play of emotions across Dante's face as he moved within her with tantalizing slowness. Despite his ardent claims to the contrary, he wasn't cold or detached. He was deeply, intensely real in every way. His kisses were like an infusion of raw need and unapologetic lust. His grip on her wrists, pinned way above her head, should have been scary, but it was simply a decadent, seductive display of his strength. Instinctively, she knew he would never hurt her. Holding her wrists like that was a game, a show of power by him, and a trusting surrender by her to the raw maleness of who he was.

Never before had sex been pure pleasure, without the threat of pain. She'd never been able to relax and not worry about what it would lead to. But in Dante's arms, shielded by the surreal strength of his frame, at the mercy of a man stronger than any she had ever known, she felt no fear. All she felt was a deliciously wonderful desire licking through her, flames that seemed to be starting in her belly and spreading outward. She loved how his eyes were darkening, becoming hooded with lust and want. "Kiss me," she whispered. "I want to feel your lips on mine."

His immediate response, swooping down to kiss her, was a heady sensation. She loved both the fact that she'd dared to tell him what she'd wanted, and that he'd given it to her. And the kiss itself was amazing. His tongue was a fiery stroke of seduction, of passion, of intimacy so private that it was like a combustible secret just for them.

Fire licked away at her, building and roiling, spreading out from her belly toward her toes and fingers. Her breath became shallow. Need crashed through her. Their kisses became more desperate and more demanding. He thrust deeper, and even deeper, withdrawing with agonizing torment and then plunging into her again, their bodies coming together in the slick, wet heat of unstoppable frenzy. More kisses, more touching, more, and more, and more—

The orgasm tore through her, dragging a scream from her throat as she arched backward, flinging herself with reckless abandon into the sensations tearing through her. Dante shouted her name, and then bucked against her, filling her with his seed as it poured out of him in a torrent of passion. Again and again the orgasm took them both, a merciless, magnificent crescendo of explosive sex, endless desire, and a relentless, eternal connection that would never release them.

Ever.

For a long time, neither of them spoke. Dante just held Elisha in his arms, their bodies tangled around each other. Her head was nestled against his shoulder, and Dante pressed his face to her hair, nuzzling the soft tresses. He'd wrapped one arm tightly around her, holding her close, while he traced small circles around her breasts with his index finger. "Your skin is so fragile," he said, unable to keep the awe out of his voice. "So soft. I'm afraid to breathe too hard or you'll shatter."

Elisha laughed softly, a throaty sound that made him smile. "How can you say that after you just made love to me like that? You weren't being careful then."

"No, I wasn't." He kissed her lightly, pretty damn certain he would never get tired of kissing her. It was kind of shocking that something that simple could be so immensely satisfying, but it was. "Are you okay?"

She smiled at him, her eyes blossoming with warmth. "Yes, you silly man, of course I am. Making love with you was the most beautiful moment I've ever experienced."

He laughed, caught up in her charm, but stupidly pleased by her comment. He liked the idea of being the one to show her what it could be like, to be the one that mattered. "You're just saying that to stroke my ego so that I'll save the world for you."

"No, I'm not." Her smile faded, and she placed her hand on his jaw. "Dante, there's so little beauty that exists. So little warmth. So little kindness. What you just gave me, I'll treasure for all my existence. It will give me the power to keep my heart open no matter how much darkness consumes me, no matter how much pain takes me."

Dante frowned at her words. "Elisha, I'm not the brightness. It's you."

She laughed softly. "It can't be me—"

"In my world, you are."

She sighed as she trailed her finger over the runes on his arm. "Then your life must have been as dark as mine."

Dark anger rolled through Dante at the thought of Elisha experiencing the kind of life he'd had, and all his peacefulness vanished. "Shit, woman, you deserve more than my life."

"As do you. You've been through so much," she mused softly.

A foreign sensation drifted through him, a sense of connection that unsettled him. He wasn't sure whether he was irritated that she'd seen his truth, or whether he liked it. "You can tell? Is it my lack of boyish charm that clued you in?"

She raised her eyebrow at him. "Well, your foot for one

thing. What happened to it?"

His eyes narrowed, not wanting to taint her or this moment with his past. The past was an albatross, contaminating the present and stripping hope from the future. "Hangnail."

She punched him lightly in the chest. "Seriously. It looks cursed."

"Cursed?" Her comment caught his interest, and he looked at her sharply. "I just figured it was poisoned. I never thought of a curse. Why do you say that?"

"Because..." It was difficult for Elisha to articulate it. She didn't have a specific reason. Now that she'd seen it close up, that had been her instinct, after all the curse damage she'd seen in her life. But maybe she was wrong. Maybe it was simply poison. Pulling out of his grasp, she sat up and gestured to his foot. "Can I touch it?"

His eyes were dark, watching her intently. He was lounging on his back with his hands locked behind his head. His biceps were flexed and one knee was cocked, showcasing parts of him that made her body radiate with heat. His sleek, muscular body completely relaxed, yet taut with vigilant readiness. "Sweetheart, there's no part of my body that's off-limits to you after what we just did."

"You're such a deviant." Her cheeks flushed, and she leaned forward to study his foot. The skin was blackened and charred. His foot and lower leg were twisted and mangled, as if every bone had been crushed and torn apart. She held her hand above it, and sharp pinpricks of pain jabbed into her palm. She sucked in her breath and turned her hand over. Sure enough, her hand was dotted with hundreds of microscopic marks, like malignant pin pricks. Fear rippled through her and she glanced at him. "I think it is cursed. What happened?"

He was watching her more intently now. His pose was the same but a new level of tension was rippling through his body. "Why do you think it's cursed?"

"Watch." She moved so she was sitting in front of him,

her legs on either side of his. Carefully, she lifted his leg onto her lap.

Dante gritted his teeth, and he bit out a curse under his breath. Beads of sweat appeared on his forehead.

"I know. Sorry." She laid her hands on either side of his ankle and gently opened her mind to his injury. Her fingers became translucent and melted through his flesh. He swore and his leg jerked, as if he had to fight to keep himself from pulling away.

"You're like ice," he said.

"It's not me," she said, as she carefully wove her fingers through his cells. "It's the damage." Slowly, ever so slowly, his foot began to shimmer and fade, becoming slightly transparent. As his skin turned the same sparkly blue of her hands, a pulsing, black shadow became visible beneath his flesh. It was moving and swirling, as if it were alive. Cold fear gripped her. "Dear God," she whispered, horrified by what she saw. "How is that possible?"

"Jesus." Dante sat up, staring at his leg. "What's that?"

"The black magic residue." Her fingers began to tremble from the effort of connecting with him, and she eased her hands out of his leg. Her whole body was shaking now, and she fisted her hands, trying to cleanse them of what she'd just touched. "How did you get this?"

"My father did it when I was fighting him. What is it?"

His *father* had done that to him? "It's a curse from beyond the nether-realm, originating in the queen's darkness." She looked at him, even as she touched his foot again, as if she could fix it by sheer strength of will. "It's made from my mother's energy, Dante. The curse is from my world."

His jaw tightened. "He cursed me? You're shitting me." Dante shouldn't have been shocked by her revelation. He'd seen his father's brutality for years. He'd known his leg was rotting from the moment his father had sliced across his ankle with a blade he'd never seen him wield before, a blade that he'd assumed had contained poison. He'd taken it as another example of what a bastard his father was, fighting with poison instead of relying on his own skills. But a curse? That was worse, because it was destruction on a whole new level, one that attacked the soul, not just the body. Anger rolled through him, fury against the man who had spent his life claiming he was a hero, when he was nothing but scum. "How do I stop it?"

"It depends on what it is. It might not be...there might not be anything you can do." She met his gaze, and her face was anguished. "But there's no way to predict. They're all different." She ran her hand over his leg again, but this time, she kept her hands corporeal. Her touch was soft and gentle, a balm that eased the throbbing in his leg. He closed his eyes, focusing entirely on her touch, on the feel of her hands on him, and on the respite she gave him. He was so used to living with the pain in his leg that it was almost shocking to feel his leg begin to relax under her soothing caress. She was doing something to his leg, and it felt incredible.

"I remember this," he said quietly, trying to force his mind away from the grim prophecy she'd just dealt him. He needed to clear his mind and stay focused if he had any chance of moving forward and finishing his last task before he died: saving the world without sacrificing Elisha.

"Remember what?"

"The feeling of being touched in kindness." Old memories surfaced, memories he'd shut down for so long, memories he'd buried out of necessity. "My mother was kind." Suddenly, he remembered her so clearly. Her blue eyes, the way she'd hugged him, the way she'd sat over his bed every night with a sword, waiting for his father to return to take him. He recalled how she'd kept them on the run, constantly moving, trying to hide from the man who she knew would be coming for Dante. "I used to have nightmares that my father had found me, and she would hold me at night and chase the demons away." He opened his eyes to see Elisha staring at him, her radiant blue-violet eyes shimmering with emotion. "Your touch is like that, too," he said quietly. "Gentle. Soothing." He grinned, a sudden, wicked gleam in his eyes. "Don't get me wrong, it's completely different than a mother's touch. But good."

She swallowed, and her palms tightened around his ankle. "What does it feel like?" she whispered. "To be touched like this?"

There was so much yearning in her voice that he forgot his own pain. "You don't know?"

She shook her head, her hair tumbling over her shoulders, even as she continued to tend to his leg. "When you kissed me, it was the first time that I've been kissed and not been afraid of what was to follow. It was amazing, and beautiful, but it was still a sexual touch, so it's different." She hesitated, and then looked down at her arm.

He could see bruises on her forearm, dark purple marks that hadn't been there before. Fierce protectiveness surged through him, and a low growl echoed deep in his chest. "Where did those come from?"

"I had them all along. I just hid them from you." She shrugged, not answering his question about how she got them. "I can control how much of my true self manifests. Will you—" She hesitated, as if uncertain whether she should ask.

She didn't have to ask. He knew what she wanted. Wordlessly, he took her hand in his and pressed a kiss to the bruises. It wasn't a sexual kiss. It was a kiss of comfort and healing, one that asked for nothing in return. She sucked in her breath, her eyes wide as she watched him. He laid his palm over her arm and focused his Calydon healing energy into the wound. A Calydon could heal only his *sheva* and other Calydons, so he knew he couldn't heal her, but they were connected enough that maybe she could feel some relief. Warmth flowed from his hand into her arm, and he stroked her bruised skin gently.

"Thank you," she said. "For showing me."

He grinned, nodding at her other hand, which was still on his damaged leg. "Feels good, doesn't it?"

She smiled. "It does."

"Maybe we should just sit here and fondle each other's injuries for the rest of the day. What do you think?"

She laughed then, a sparkly laugh that seemed to light up the night. "I think that's a great idea. The world can save itself, don't you think?"

"Shit, I wish it could."

Her smile faded, and her eyes became heavy with wisdom. "I'm sorry you had to kill your father."

He was startled by her comment. He would have expected her to condemn him for it. Good sons didn't murder their fathers. "You understand?"

She shrugged, still touching his leg, as if she were getting as much comfort from it as he was, which he understood, because he was happy as hell to be running his fingers down her arm. He'd never felt skin so soft in his life, and he hadn't been lying when he said he'd be down with just parking his ass on the ground with her and not moving again. He was tired of all the crap. He was tired of watching so many people die. He was just tired. "My mother is the queen of darkness," she said simply. "I understand about parents who hurt their children."

"I wish you didn't." Dante grasped her wrist and tugged her against him. She came willingly, sliding into his arms as if she'd been waiting for him to reach for her. Outside the realm of their little cocoon, he could feel the sword still calling to him, but with Elisha tucked up against him, it couldn't control him. He knew they had to make decisions and take action, but being in Elisha's arms gave him a respite to clear his head and focus, and he needed that right now.

He kissed the top of her head, knowing that reality was too damn close. "How long until I die?"

"I don't know. We never know, do we?"

He laughed at her philosophical answer. "I was looking

for something a little more specific, given the rate at which my leg is decaying."

"It's a bad one," she said simply. "Very bad." She propped her elbow on his chest so she could look at him. Her brow was furrowed with worry. "How would your father have gotten access to my mother's curses? What was he like?"

"What was he like? Shit, that's a story."

"I need to know. If my mother has found a way to contaminate the earth..." Fear flickered in her eyes. "Dante, we need to know. The sword I understand, but if she has other tentacles, the situation could be more critical." Fear tightened her voice, and he instinctively wrapped his arms more tightly around her, pulling her into his embrace. Even as he did so, he reached out with his preternatural senses, assessing their surroundings. No longer was he searching simply for the threat of another being. He was looking for that dark, sinister energy that he knew all too well, the one that had bled from his father as he'd watched him die.

Shit. He didn't want to talk about this father. The bastard was dead and needed to be cast aside. But Elisha was right. They needed to know what the situation was. They needed to know if there was more of the same coming after them. He took a deep breath and pulled Elisha closer, as if her presence could block the poison of memories long past while he dredged up the memories of who his father had been. "One hundred and ten years ago, I had my dream," he told her, trailing his fingers through her hair, recalling the story that best exemplified his father. "The one in which a young Calydon has a battle with death in his sleep. If he triumphs, he awakens with his brands and becomes a Calydon. If he fails, he dies in his sleep."

Elisha frowned, her forehead puckering. "I take it you survived."

"I did." He kissed her wrinkles away as he spoke, somehow needing to touch her, to get respite from his words. "I awoke to find my father's dagger in my chest, hilt-deep."

Elisha gasped and sat up, staring at him. "He tried to murder you when you survived the dream?"

Her outrage on his behalf made something in his chest shift, like a knife that had been lodged in there for so long had suddenly begun to work itself free. "He wanted to make sure I was tough enough to be Order. Surviving the dream wasn't enough. I had to survive *him*. He'd had one son before me, a warrior with great potential who hadn't survived his dream. My father was the only Order member who hadn't sired a son who'd made it into the Order, and it made him crazed. He wanted to make sure I was tough enough, so he started training me when I was five." If one could classify the abuse he'd taken as training.

Elisha was staring at him, her hand over her heart, as if she could feel the blade that his father had shoved into his chest. "What did you do after he stabbed you?"

"Fought him." He shrugged. "I didn't win. He was going to kill me for being too weak to defeat him, but another Calydon named Louis intervened." Louis had been only three years older than him, still young enough to think for himself. "My father was impressed that I had attracted a powerful ally, so he decided to let me live and induct me into the Order." He stared at the night sky, remembering that hell. "My first task was to lead the team into a nearby village and rape six women. I was supposed to go back in five years and see if I'd spawned any boys so we could take them and train them."

Elisha shook her head in denial of his words. "You didn't do that, did you? I know you didn't."

"No. I left." He would never forget that moment that he walked away. Or, rather, dragged himself away. Once his father had realized Dante was leaving, he'd attacked. It had been brutal, leaving Dante crawling across the ground, his life bleeding out with each passing second. "He tried to cut my weapons out of my flesh, and my heart out of my body. He said I didn't deserve to be a Calydon. He thought he'd killed me, and left me for dead."

Tears burned in Elisha's eyes, tears so stark with grief that he knew that his story was reminding her of her own life, of her own mother. "Parents shouldn't hurt their children," she whispered.

"No, they shouldn't." He hugged her tightly and pressed a kiss to her forehead. "Maybe that's why your mom and my dad decided to work together. They had so much in common."

Elisha shook her head, as if to clear the thoughts of their parents from her mind. "You didn't die," she said, pulling their focus back to his story and away from her own nightmares.

"No, I'm not that agreeable." He remembered how he'd sprawled in that dirt for days, fading in and out of the Calydon healing sleep. "There was a light. A golden light—"

Her eyes widened, and she sat up again, watching him with an expression of awe on her face. "An angel came to help you?"

"Maybe." He felt weird admitting that he'd been rescued by an angel. It felt like his own secret, a whisper that had been shared only with him. He'd never told anyone, not until that moment, but it felt right to share it with Elisha. He remembered that feeling of impotence after his father's attack. He'd been unable to fight, to stand, and he'd known he'd been dying, until that light had come. "I never saw the person with the light, but I sensed a woman. An angel, I'm sure of it."

Elisha smiled. "I'm so glad she came for you. How can you say that you're not a good man? Angels don't give their golden light to those who are undeserving."

He shrugged, not wanting to delude himself that he had some higher purpose in this world. "Well, the angel saved my life, but even with her help, it took me almost a month to recover from what he did to me." He'd managed to crawl away, finally, and then...

He stopped, that scene screaming before his eyes again, that moment when the hell he'd left behind came crashing back. "I was wandering aimlessly after that. I had no focus. Then, a few months later, I was in a village, and I saw one of the team raping a woman in the middle of the square. I knew my father had sent him. I lost all discipline and control when I saw him with her. I couldn't allow it to happen anymore."

Elisha's eyes flashed in anger at his father. "What happened?"

Dante laughed bitterly. "Then things got bad." That was when he learned what hell really was. That was when he changed from a rebellious kid to a man with one mission. That was when he'd made his choice. That was when he'd crossed the line and become the killer his father had always wanted him to be.

CHAPTER SEVEN

Elisha felt the tension churn through Dante, and she sat up. His face was dark with swirling emotions, his fists clenched. His father had tried to murder him twice, and *that* wasn't the bad part? A cold chill ran through her at the idea of what it must have felt like to wake up with his father's dagger in his chest. The betrayal by a parent was like a bleeding wound that never healed, no matter what. She knew that, because she lived it every day. Was it any wonder that she'd connected with Dante so completely from the first moment? They were the same. She didn't have to hear the rest of Dante's story to know that he'd stopped the Order member from raping that woman. She knew that he had, no matter what the cost. It was what came after that had shaped him. "What happened after you killed him?"

Dante leaned forward, his arms draped over his knees as he sat hunched over, like he could ward off the memories through his stance. He laughed bitterly. "It turned out that the woman was the daughter of a king who had paid the bastard to rape her."

A cold sweat broke out on Elisha's shoulders and trickled down her back. "Why?" she whispered. "Why do parents do that to their daughters?" She couldn't keep the pain out of her voice, and she couldn't hide the trembling of her hands.

Memories flashed through her mind, memories she tried so hard never to acknowledge. Hands that hurt. Dark rooms. Chains. Fear beyond what words could ever express.

Dante turned sharply to look at her, and then his face softened. "Your mother handed you off like that, didn't she?"

Elisha nodded once, her throat too tight to speak.

"Jesus." Dante's face turned ashen, and he pulled her into his arms. For a moment, neither of them spoke. He just held her, and she buried herself against his strong bulk. She knew it didn't make sense, but somehow, being in Dante's arms made her feel like all the terrible things in her life had happened to someone else. It was as if he gave her the strength to put up a shield between herself and her life, and to strip it of the power to hurt her. "Someday," he said quietly, his breath warm and comforting against her skin, "I'm going to kill your mother for you."

His casual tone evoked a strangled laugh from her, and she looked up at him. "You're a good man."

"Nope." His voice was calm, but there was a deadly edge to it that made chills run down her arms. "I'm a vicious, bloodthirsty bastard, and I'm very much looking forward to the day that I watch your mother's head roll across the floor."

She had to laugh this time, such dangerous words spoken with such casualness. He was so matter-of-fact, but at the same time, she knew he meant it. And honestly, she appreciated it. No man had ever been bold enough to consider killing her mother. It was definitely the sweetest thing anyone had ever said to her. "Thank you. That's very heroic of you."

He met her gaze. "I'm deadly serious. It might not be until after I'm dead, but I'll make it happen." His face darkened, and sudden heat seemed to burn from the brands on his forearms. "And the men who hurt you, too. Every last one of them will know what it's like to suffer before he dies. I promise you that."

Her throat tightened, and she nodded, words suddenly sticking in her throat. She'd never had an ally before, and it was really beautiful. She didn't believe in hurting others, in revenge, in retribution, but she couldn't deny that Dante's words sounded so beautiful to her. He made her feel like she didn't have to be afraid, like those who had hurt her were not inviolable, that maybe she didn't have to be the victim anymore, even if it was simply in her own mind and her own memories. "You're going to make me cry. No one has ever offered to kill for me before. It's really sweet." She couldn't keep the tears out of her voice. God, was she pathetic or what? One sincere offer to murder on her behalf and she got all weepy?

A slow, half-grin crept across Dante's face. "Well, hey, if I'm going to run around killing people, I might as well include a few that deserve it, huh?" He cocked an eyebrow. "Unless you want the honor? I'm happy to set it up for you and let you deal the final blow."

Elisha had a momentary vision of the people who had hurt her sprawled across the ground, and she shuddered. "No," she whispered. "I can't do that."

"Then I will. People who hurt women and innocents don't deserve second chances." The edge was back in his voice, and she knew that he was thinking of that night so long ago when he'd killed to save that girl his former teammate was trying to rape.

She wanted to hear a happy ending. She wanted to hear about a girl who got away. "What happened to the girl? Did you stop him in time?" She couldn't keep the tremble out of her voice, and Dante took her hand in his.

"Sweetheart, she was okay. I got there in time, and I will always get there in time for you, too. Okay?"

Tears filled her eyes, and she nodded. "You saved her." A girl had been protected from that fate. Maybe it was one woman, one time, but it gave her hope. "Why would her father do that to her? I don't understand."

Dante snorted in disgust as he ran his hand down her arm, a gesture that eased some of the tension from her. "He'd allied with my father to create a well-funded Order. My father wanted some good lineage and money, and the king wanted a grandson who was as powerful as an Order member. Together, they figured they could spawn an entire army, and they were both pissed as hell at me. Since I wasn't agreeable enough to die once they caught me, the king had me thrown into a pit of hell. My father helped him do it."

A pit of hell? The tension in his voice pricked a memory in Elisha's mind, a rumor that she'd heard many years ago about the one place on earth that was almost as bad as the world she grew up in. But it couldn't be. Not for Dante. "Not... Orion's Pit? That's not what you were in, was it?"

His eyebrows went up. "You've heard of it?"

A cold chill rippled over her. "Yes." Dear God, she'd heard about that pit. Two hundred feet deep, and eighty feet wide at the base. The only sunlight and water that penetrated was that which filtered through a large grate at the top. Anyone or any otherworld creature who displeased the king was thrown in there, fully armed, into a brutal world where the only food was the bodies of the other prisoners. It was a fight to survive, every minute of every day. Her mother had idolized it and created her own imitation of it, just because she was so inspired by it. Elisha would never forget the screams of the people trapped inside, or the scent of death and carnage that constantly emanated from it...and Dante had lived it. "That's where you were? How long were you there?"

"One hundred years."

Her hand went to her mouth in shock. "Oh, God." What had he been forced to do to survive all that time? "Dante, I'm so sorry."

"Yeah." Dante shifted restlessly and flexed his hands, which she suddenly noticed had scars across the backs of them. Instinctively, she clasped his hands in hers, and he immediately closed his fingers around hers. He leaned forward, searching her face with tormented eyes, as if by sharing his past with her he could make it go away. "I saw shit that I had never even realized existed, Elisha. I learned to kill without remorse or hesitation. I learned to stand over the body of another living creature and watch its life bleed from its mangled body. I learned how to go weeks without ever going to sleep. I saw how truly bad men could be, but I also realized that there was one big difference between my father and all the murderers in that pit: my father had a choice not to be like that, and he did it anyway. These men were brutal, but they were doing it to survive. It was in that pit that I realized the full depths of how bad the Order of the Blade had become."

She wanted to cry for him, her heart breaking for what he must have lived through, for the lessons he had learned in that hell. Orion's pit had turned a gallant, idealistic youth into a warrior beyond his endurance and comprehension, a man with a mission. No wonder the sword had chosen him. No wonder he'd been able to let go of it. No wonder he had become the man he now was. "How did you survive?"

"A warrior named Rohan was dropped in there the same day I was. He and I both wanted to live, and we had no other allies." He grinned, but there was no laughter in his eyes. "Without each other, we both would have died." This time, a faint hint of warmth softened his eyes. "Rohan taught me the value of having one person at your back who you could trust at all times."

She managed a smile, her heart warming for this warrior she'd never met. She knew what it was like to have one person to count on. She'd had her faerie. Dante had found Rohan. "Well, I'll have to meet Rohan someday and thank him for keeping you alive."

"It was a mutual effort," he said. "I don't think Rohan would have stood by me unless I gave him as much as he gave me. We needed each other." He stared up at the sky, and she followed his glance.

The night was full of stars, stars that she knew he hadn't

been able to see while trapped, stars she'd never seen until she'd escaped from the queen's darkness. "They're beautiful, aren't they?"

"They're freedom," he agreed. "I never thought I'd see them again. I thought I'd spend the rest of my life in there. Rohan is a good man, but I have to admit, it got old sleeping with him every night."

"I imagine it did." She leaned against him and rested her head on his shoulder, drained by their discussion. She felt like she'd relived her own nightmares and experienced the pit with him. How could they both have lived such darkness, only to find each other and this moment? "How did you get out?" No one ever got out. They stayed in there until they died. To survive for one hundred years was incredible. To escape was impossible. And yet he'd done both.

For a split second, real hope flared in her heart, hope that maybe, somehow, this whole nightmare could turn out okay. Dante had accomplished the impossible before. Why not one more time? But even as she thought it, she knew it was a lost hope. Some things took more than courage and strength, no matter how much of it one had. There was no easy answer to what they were facing. Even now, she could feel the swirling energy of the sword still summoning Dante, like a relentless pulsing that would not be denied.

"A kid was dropped through the grill one night," Dante said, answering her question as he entwined his fingers with hers and pressed a kiss to each of her knuckles, as if trying to ground himself in their present instead of his past. His gaze flicked restlessly toward the sword, and then he blinked in surprise. "It moved."

She looked over and saw that the sword had indeed pried itself free of the tree, and it was now back in its pool, lying in wait for Dante, summoning him. The fact that it had returned to its place of power was indicative of just how strong it was. She knew he was feeling its compulsion. Grimacing, she touched Dante's arm, trying to draw his focus away from it. "Tell me about this boy?"

Dante dragged his gaze off the sword and looked at her, his face grim. "He was skinny, maybe fifteen years old at most, by far the youngest person I'd ever seen in there. He was unconscious and half-dead, and the crew converged upon him. He was going to be dinner in a second."

A child had been sent into that hell? A child who had been gifted with Dante as a protector. It made her sad, so sad, to know that some of the darkness she lived with in the queen's realm gripped the earth as well…except that men like Dante were there to stop it from taking over. She snuggled closer to him. "You protected him." It wasn't a question. She knew the answer.

Dante shrugged and looped his free arm around her, tucking her closer against him. He rested his head against hers, watching as she played with his fingers. It was an intimate, peaceful moment, despite the topic. It was almost as if their mingled presence could ward off the darkness of their lives. "He was a kid. He deserved a chance, so yeah, Rohan and I stood guard. It took him almost two months to wake up."

"Two months? Was he in a coma or something?"

"I don't know. He never moved, but we could tell he was still breathing. Then one day…" He paused, as if he were reliving the event. "A major storm rolled through the area. Ten minutes into it, the kid woke up. Just opened his eyes and looked at Rohan and me. He said one word, 'Help,' and pointed at the side of the pit. We grabbed him, hauled him to his feet, and dragged him over to the wall. He slammed his hands onto it, and then the storm unleashed its fury right down into the pit. Lightning. Thunder. Rain. Wind. Then the entire place crumbled. The earth literally gave out and buried every person, except for Rohan, the kid, and me. When it was over, the pit was open to the sky, and the grate was gone. The kid turned to us and told us his name was Vaughn. He thanked us for protecting him, and then hauled ass up the rocks and disappeared. We went up after him, and that was it. We were out, and he was gone."

"He saved you, as you saved him." Tears brimmed in her eyes for these warriors who had stood beside each other even when surrounded by the dregs of survival, by a life that allowed for no compassion. Warriors who had retained their humanity despite all they'd endured...exactly as she'd fought so hard to do in her own life, refusing to succumb to the darkness that surrounded her.

Dante shook his head. "Maybe. I don't know. I've replayed that night in my head a thousand times, and I'm still not sure what happened, or whether he caused it." He twisted a lock of her hair around his finger, and then gently brushed it back from her face, a gesture so tender she wanted to cry. "But when I got out that night, I didn't even care. I was just so damn happy to be free. I can't even tell you what it was like to breathe fresh air again, and to feel the wind on my face."

She smiled in understanding. "I know, because that's what I felt like when I arrived here. It's incredible. I don't think you can appreciate the simplicity of freedom until you've suffered." She relaxed against him and rested her hand on his leg, needing to hear the rest of his story, somehow needing to understand the complexity of what drove this man that was so pivotal to the future of the earth. "So, that's when you went after your father?"

He nodded. "When I found him, he struck first. He didn't wait to find out why I was there. He just tried to kill me." He gave a bitter laugh. "One hundred years in the pit made me a better opponent than he was anticipating. Score one for the underachieving son."

She smiled sadly for the small victories in his life. "That's when he cursed you?"

"Yeah. I didn't get the chance to talk to him much. He was carrying a sword I hadn't seen before, and that's what he used. The sword was curved with rubies in the handle." He raised his brows. "Sound familiar?"

She shook her head. "Was he with anyone?"

"Alone. I don't know what he'd been doing that whole time, though."

Elisha bit her lip in frustration. How had his father gotten that cursed sword? "What happened next?"

Dante shrugged. "After I killed him, I hunted down every other member of the Order. After you've killed once, it gets easier." He held out his hands, as if showing her the blood he could still see on them. "I killed them as ruthlessly as they had killed so many others. I did my job, Elisha. I shut down my emotions so I could kill them all in cold blood. One by one, I watched them die, all to save the innocents. I stood over their bodies, and I didn't care." His voice was grim, weighted, and she knew he was lying to himself when he'd claimed not to care.

It had affected him deeply to have killed so many men that had been a part of his life, including his father. "You do care," she said softly. "And it's okay."

"No. I can't afford to care," he said wearily. "Don't you get it? A warrior has to be ruthless and cold, focused on what he has to do. When they care, about a woman, about power, about revenge, that's when they become vulnerable to corruption."

"It's not true. If you care, that makes you stronger. That's why you could kill your own father, because you *do* care about the right things. You cared about him, but you cared more about the people he was hurting. If you care, then you make the right choice, no matter how difficult it is."

"Really?" He turned toward her suddenly, his eyes blazing with frustration and exhaustion. "And what's the right choice this time, Elisha? Killing you to keep the earth safe? Really? I'm supposed to destroy the one good thing I've ever found in my life? Because, I'll tell you, keeping you alive is what I care about now. Not doing the right thing. I want to use my power to save *you*. I'm not man enough to make the choice to sacrifice you to save the world." He bowed his head, fisting his hands until the muscles in his shoulders bulged. "I can't do this anymore," he whispered. "I'm done killing. I'm done making that choice. I can't sit here and shut it down anymore. I can't be the focused, stoic warrior that I have to be." He ran his hand through his hair in an anguished move. "You can't die. Others can't die." He raised his head, and she saw the stark anguish in his eyes. "The one thing I swore to do was to make the world safe for innocents. Destroying the sword is the last thing I have to do before I die, and I can't do it, because I can't hurt you."

His voice almost broke with the anguish of his words, his pain was so great. Tears filled her eyes, and she shook her head. "I don't want to die either," she whispered. "Not since I met you. It's so much harder when you care. I know it is."

Her confession seemed to deflate him, and he sank back on his heels and closed his eyes, as if willing control back into his body. Together, they sat in silence, each of them trying to catch their breath. Finally, Dante opened his eyes. They were blood-shot and turbulent. "I can't let the earth be destroyed."

She shook her head. "No, we can't."

"I can't sacrifice you."

Fresh tears brimmed. "Dante, we have to do what's right. It's not about us. This is bigger than us—"

"No. I'm tired of everything being bigger than what I want." He fisted his hand, and then there was a crack and a flash of black light. His spear appeared in his hand, and he laid it on the ground. "No more innocents die because of my choices. No more sacrifice for the greater good. No more of my father's values."

She bit her lip to fight back the words her heart wanted to say. She wanted to fall into his arms, to hide from the choices they had to make, and to let this man who was saying such incredible words have what he wanted, because it was what she wanted, too. "It's not your father's values," she said. "It's the mission of the Order. It was distorted by your father, but it is right. Sometimes those choices have to be made—"

"No!" With a roar of outrage, he grabbed the spear and hurled it across the clearing. It slammed into a rock and buried itself deep into the granite boulder. He whirled around to face her, his muscles vibrating with tension. "There was no way out of that pit, and we found one. So, we're going to find another way this time as well."

She wanted to cover her ears and protect herself from his words. "Stop it! It's not fair to either of us to create false hope. There isn't a chance for a happy ending—"

He grabbed her shoulders, his eyes blazing. "You don't get it, Elisha. I can't let one more innocent die. Not you. Not the world. It will destroy me. It ends now. *There has to be another way.*"

Frustration tore through her. "What way, Dante? Do you have another Vaughn who can show up and bring down the sky? Or Rohan, who will stand by your back and cheer you to victory? Because if there's a way, I'm game, but not at the risk of destroying the earth—" She stopped, startled by the sudden look of shock on Dante's face. "What?"

"Rohan," he whispered. "*Rohan.*" There was sudden, desperate hope on his face. "He was able to train me on the protective runes because Calydons are driven by demon magic. Rohan can manipulate it. He has a connection to the nether-realm. What if he can help us? What if he can read the sword?"

Hope leapt through her. Was there really someone who could help them? "Read it? What do you mean?"

"He's a seer, Elisha. He can see the future, and other possibilities." He slammed his fist into his palm, excitement rippling off him. "He might be able to help. Or..." He cut himself off, staring grimly at her.

The hope that had alighted in her heart crashed just as

quickly at Dante's expression. "Or *what*?"

"Or he might kill you on sight."

Elisha tensed. "Why?"

"Because you're of the nether-realm, or beyond it. He has little tolerance for that kind of darkness." He gritted his teeth and turned away, swearing under his breath. "He's sworn to protect the earth from the nether-realm. You are that which he lives to destroy."

Well, that was just not helpful. "Then we can't do it. We can't call him." She shook her head. "It's not worth the risk. I need to stay alive to stop you if you won't destroy the sword."

"To stop me?" With a low growl, Dante swung around, grabbed her by the wrist, and yanked her against him.

She stiffened at the feel of his bare chest against hers, but at the same time, need for him flooded her so intensely she sucked in her breath. It hadn't been sated by their lovemaking, or by the weight of their reality. Simply being in his arms again made desire pour over her just as strongly. In truth, it had become more intense, more powerful, and more ruthless. His eyes churned with desire, and she felt his cock rise hard and fast against her belly, making desire roil through her.

Whatever was between them was mutual, and dangerous. Between the sword and his own need for her, the danger was mounting, drawing them ruthlessly closer to the vortex of doom. "Tell me, Elisha, could you really kill me? Can you? If I walked up there, shredded the veil, and then stood aside to let the worlds collide, would you kill me?"

She stared at him, horrible emotions warring within her. Could she really kill him? Could she really sink her dagger into his chest? She had to. That was why she'd come, to stop the sword's chosen from wielding it. Silently, wordlessly, she nodded. "Yes," she whispered. "If that is what it takes, then yes."

"Yes?" Betrayal darkened his eyes, and guilt tore at her. "The woman who burns in my veins so fiercely could kill me?

Do I not burn in yours?"

"Yes, yes, but—"

"The *sheva* bond," he growled. "They are fated to bond," he recited as he slid his hand over her lower back and pulled her more tightly against him. "Once that bond is complete, he will go rogue, and the only one who can stop him is his *sheva*, who will kill him." He looked at her. "You would kill me? To stop me? Just like a *sheva*."

"I'm not your *sheva,* but yes, I would." But even as she said her strong words, the truth ate at her soul, and she shook her head in despair. "I don't know," she admitted. "I might simply stand there while you brought down the veil. I don't know if I can kill you anymore, even to save the earth."

Her words hung like a dark threat between them.

"I can't resist the sword forever," he said, looking over his shoulder at the weapon. "It will summon me, and I will take it to the veil. If I'm unable destroy it because I won't sacrifice you, and you won't kill me either, then it wins."

Elisha swallowed, the reality of their situation staring at her too vividly. "So, we have only one chance."

Dante nodded grimly as he called his spear back from the boulder. It thudded into his hand, and he gripped it tightly. "We must call Rohan."

CHAPTER EIGHT

The afternoon sunlight stretched long, too long. Time was running out as Dante moved quickly, setting up the rocks in formation with such swiftness and perfection that Elisha suspected he had done it many times before. He was building a pentagram, carved in the earth, the corners each anchored by a sharp rock in the shape of an arrowhead. Dante had explained it was how he needed to call Rohan, but with each passing moment, she became more anxious. What if Rohan killed her? What if he couldn't help? They were running out of time.

With each rock Dante set in place, the air grew thicker and heavier, tainted by darkness that Elisha was all too familiar with, making her restless. She could feel the power of the sword growing, summoning Dante, and she could feel the effort he was expending not to grab it. She glanced at the nearby mountain, and saw a puff of black and purple steam plume from the top, cascading down the rocky sides as if the smoke was heavier than the air itself, as if it were carrying debris and dragging it down onto the surface. She shivered as she watched it. The mountain was coming alive, sensing the impending severing of the veil. The situation was unfolding with pre-fated precision.

She touched Dante's arm. "The barrier to the nether-realm is thinning," she told him. "I can feel it coming through."

Not just the nether-realm, but taint from the queen's darkness. She shivered, unable to keep herself from looking around, half expecting the creatures of the night to start emerging from the shadows.

"I know." Dante stood back and called out his spear with a crack and a flash of black light. He dragged the tip across his palm, carving a thick gash in his hand. "I need your blood, too."

"Mine?" Elisha shook her head, knowing all too well the cost of allowing someone to control her through her blood. "No, I can't—"

"If Rohan's going to see for both of us, we need to build a conduit for both of us." He held out his hand. "Come."

She stared at him. "Isn't the blood bond one of the stages of the *sheva* bond? What if we accidentally—"

"It won't matter. We're both protected." He nodded at the runes still burned into his flesh.

Elisha glanced nervously toward the pool where the sword was resting. The water had started boiling an hour ago, and she knew it would not be long before it claimed Dante. In her pocket lay the Blade of Cormoranth...but even as she thought it, she looked at Dante, at his dark eyes, at his strong stance. He was a warrior of such honor. Was there really a chance she could kill him?

No, no, there was not. Was he strong enough to destroy the sword? No one was, but at the same time, Dante gave her hope. There was so much honor in him, so much goodness... but if he did it, she would die. And as she looked at this man who had made love to her, for the first time in her life, she became afraid of death. She became afraid of what she would lose if she died. She had just met this man, but he had changed everything for her. For the first time in her life, she knew tenderness and warmth, and it was because of him.

If she died, it would be over. Dante would be over. Just the thought of being separated from him made anguish pulse in her heart, and she realized she didn't want to die. And with that realization, all her power left her. If she was afraid to die, what did she have left? Nothing. Her willingness to sacrifice her own life to stop her mother had always been Elisha's only tool against her. But Dante had taken that from her.

What had she done?

He held out his hand for hers. "Elisha?"

She had to try. Wordlessly, she held out her hand. Dante took her hand in his and pressed his lips to her palm. "I'm sorry to have to do this, Elisha."

She nodded. "I know."

Without taking his gaze off hers, he took his spear and swiped it across her palm. She jumped at the stab of pain, and he immediately pressed his lips to the wound, taking away her pain. She smiled sadly at his tender gesture. The man kissed her bleeding hand to make her feel better? "You're not making it easy for me to kill you if I need to," she muttered.

He grinned, a smile that seemed to light up her heart. "I know. I'm difficult that way." He clasped her hand with his injured one. "Let's do this—"

A searing pain ricocheted through her hand as their blood mingled. She yelped and tried to jerk her hand free, but he didn't let go, his grip tight around hers as he went down on his knees, still gripping her hand. Pain was etched on the lines of his face, and she knew he was feeling the same shock. "Let go!" she demanded, trying to pull free of his grasp. The pain was excruciating, traveling up her arm as if her very blood had been contaminated by his.

"I can't," he gritted out. He pulled on her hand, tugging her down to her knees in front of him. His fist went to her hair and he yanked her close, his face inches from hers. "I have to say it," he growled. "I can't stop myself."

"Say what?" But even as she asked, she knew. The words were in her head, screaming at her. Words she didn't recognize, but somehow knew.

He dragged her up against him, so her breasts were against his chest. "Mine to you. Yours to me. Bonded by blood, by spirit and by soul, we are one. No distance too far, no enemy too powerful, no sacrifice too great. I'll always find you. I'll always protect you. No matter what the cost. I am yours as you are mine." He bit out the words, almost angry, and they hammered at her, assaulting her, like a fierce wind trying to rip her to shreds.

Rightness filled her, like a great burst of sunlight. Then she heard herself saying the words in her own head, the words she didn't want, the words she didn't even know. "Mine to you. Yours to me. Bonded by blood, by spirit and by soul, we are one. No distance too far, no enemy too powerful, no sacrifice too great. I'll always find you. I'll always keep you safe. No matter what the cost. I am yours as you are mine."

Dante growled with possession and anger, even as he pulled her against him and kissed her. It was a frantic, desperate kiss that exploded through her. Equally desperate, she threw her arms around him and kissed him back, needing his touch, needing to feel his body against hers, needing more. The words they'd pledged continued to echo through her mind, evoking a need for Dante beyond what she'd ever felt before.

He grabbed her by the hips, and shoved his hands under her dress, even as he kissed her. "God, yes," she whispered, grappling for the front of his pants. The moment she freed him, he yanked her against him, sheathing himself inside her so fiercely she screamed at the invasion.

He gripped her hair, holding her at his mercy as he kissed her, ruthless possessive kisses of ownership...and it felt so right. She, the woman who would give herself to no man, burned for the way he was claiming her. He drove deep, one arm locked around her waist, holding her against him as he buried himself in her again and again. Elisha locked her legs around his hips, her body writhing as he drove into her, her gasps of agonized pleasure swallowed by kisses that tore through all her shields, exposing her all the way down to her core.

It became too much, the lovemaking, the passion, the *need*, making her ache and writhe for more, for completion. With a roar, Dante staggered to his feet and slammed her against a tree trunk, bracing her against the trunk. She gripped his shoulders, gasping as he drove into her, his hands tight on her hips as he held her relentlessly, holding her where he wanted her, staking his claim on her with every thrust, every kiss, every move. Harder and harder he drove into her, and she screamed as desire built within her, twisting her and tormenting her until it was beyond what she could withstand. "Dante," she gasped, "I can't—"

"We can—" Then he drove again, a final time, and the orgasm exploded through her. Her body went rigid, and colors exploded through her mind. Red, green, violet, yellow, ruthless swirls of energy trying to consume her as fire rushed through her body, igniting every cell.

Dante shouted her name and then bucked against her, impaling himself so deeply within her that she knew they would never part, that their connection would hold them in its ruthless grasp for all eternity. His body went rigid, his grip on her merciless as he fought to help them both survive the orgasm terrorizing them both. The orgasm was not relief, and it did not end. It grew and grew, consuming them. It was ruthless, devastating, too much, too much... "Stay with me, Elisha," he shouted, his voice barely penetrating the kaleidoscope of colors and noise that was pressing down upon her.

He kissed her again, and this time, through the din, she felt him reach for her, not just with his hands, but with his soul. His energy rushed through her, and she lunged for his strength, opening her spirit to him. They connected instantly, and he enfolded her in his spirit, immediately weaving a protective shield around them both. The orgasm hammered at his protections like a predator, streaking through them, rattling everything, fighting to tear them apart. Elisha buried her face in Dante's shoulder, clinging to him as he pressed his body into her, using his strength to hold them up, to hold them together, locking them in a defensive embrace, just trying to survive the assault, but it was too much, too powerful—

Elisha. His voice was like a warm flood of strength through her soul, a gasp of air.

Dante? She thought his name and felt his response instantly.

Focus on me, Elisha. I've got us. Again, his voice seemed to caress her, encircling her mind with power and protection.

Elisha held tight to that sound, the feel of his spirit, huddling against him as the waves of the orgasm continued to blast them, tearing at them, weakening her until all she could do was focus on the feel of Dante's body still pinning her against the tree, on the warmth of his spirit, on the sound of his voice still talking to her...until suddenly, abruptly, mercifully, it was over.

Every muscle in his body was shaking violently.

His breath rasped in his chest, as if it were tearing flesh each time he inhaled.

His blood burned where it flowed through his veins.

Every part of his body hurt from the orgasm.

And he could tell from the way Elisha was trembling that he'd failed to protect her from the same fate. He pressed his face into her hair, his arms still locked around her, his cock still deep inside her. Her legs were clamped around his hips as she gripped his shoulders, her face buried in the curve of his neck. *Elisha?*

She didn't respond, and he couldn't find her in his mind. Had he imagined their mental connection? Shit, he hoped he had. Or hadn't. He didn't even know what had just happened between them. He just knew it was dangerous as hell. "Elisha?"

This time, he spoke aloud.

She groaned. "What just happened? And don't tell me it was simply because you're a Calydon, because I won't believe it. Even you guys can't produce an endless orgasm that sucks all the life out of you before you have a chance to brag to all your friends."

He laughed softly at her disbelieving tone. "Maybe it was a warning by the gods never to have sex again?"

"It worked." She lifted her head from his shoulder, and he saw pain etched in her eyes. "I thought I was going to burn up from the inside out. It was as if lightning was searing me."

"I know. Me, too." He had to look at her arm. He knew he had to check to see if she was carrying his brand. The blood bond had compelled their intimacy, and that would happen only with a *sheva*. And the sex...had that been driven by the blood bond, or had it been something else? Because he'd never heard of the blood bond inducing that kind of response. He had to know what he was dealing with and look for the brand that would indicate their fate. But as hell was his witness, he didn't want to.

"What were those words we said?" She looked up, so much exhaustion in those violet-blue eyes. She no longer carried the sated look of a woman well-loved. It was the haunted expression of a woman barely hanging on, trying to regain control of the situation, of herself. But there was no blame or recrimination in her eyes, just the need to reach for him for comfort and understanding.

He ground his jaw at her question, knowing that the blame would appear on her face when he told her the truth. "Those words are the oath from the blood bond stage of the *sheva* bond."

Her eyes went wide, and she jerked her arm from his neck and looked down. He followed her gaze, but his brand was not on her arm. They were still safe. Relief cascaded through him, and he closed his eyes for a long moment, willing strength back into his body. "We're still good." Except he knew that they weren't. Calydons could talk mind-to-mind only with other Calydons, except in the case of their soul mate. "Did you...hear my voice in your head while we were making love?"

She nodded. "Yes, but I can't anymore."

"Shit." He didn't know what was going on, but they both needed space right now. He palmed her hips, supporting her as he withdrew, both of them gasping as he pulled out. The orgasm hit again, and he grimaced, fighting to retain control as Elisha bucked in his arms. He held her tightly, their cheeks pressed together as they clung to each other, their bodies screaming as the orgasm tore through them with even more ferocity than the first time. It was ruthless, merciless, violent, taking them over yet again. He drilled his focus down, fighting to protect them, to somehow shield them from the repeated onslaught. But he couldn't halt it, and it raked through them again, even though he wasn't even inside her.

She screamed, and he caught her mouth in a kiss, desperate to find a way out of the loop. *Elisha, we have to ride it. We can't fight it. It's stronger than us.* Instinctively, he reached for her mind again, and this time, he felt her awareness when he touched her mind.

I can't, Dante. It's too much. It hurts—

Stop fighting it. Give yourself over to me. Just let me absorb the pain. We have to try it. Come on! He kissed her face, kissed away the tears streaming down her cheeks, even as he tightened his grip on her hips, fighting to hold her against him, struggling to protect her from the bark that was against her back. He tried to back up, to pull her away from the trunk, but he couldn't do it. The orgasm held them both too ruthlessly, howling through him like a demon possessed. *We can't beat it. We have to go with it.*

He kissed her again, using all his strength and control not to hurt her, when his entire being was screaming at him to take her, to consume her, to tear her very soul from her body. Sweat poured down him as he fought to keep the kiss gentle, seductive, his muscles screaming in agony as he kept his grip gentle. *Just let me love you, Elisha. Just let it take you. I'll protect you. I swear it.* He eased inside her again, her body so slick and wet for him.

Elisha gasped as he entered her, and he felt her body convulsing as the orgasm increased in intensity. He moved slowly, so agonizingly slowly, fighting to seduce, to coax, to be the slow lover who wouldn't rip his woman to shreds. *My sweet Elisha,* he whispered as he kissed her, as he drove inside her, a move that made him bellow in response as the orgasm spasmed through him *yet again*. His seed spilled forth, but he was still hard, still driving into her, still desperate.

Dante, help me. She was gripping him so tightly, her body convulsing. *It won't stop. It won't.*

Swearing, Dante drove again, and again, and Elisha writhed on his cock, sending them both into further frenzies. She was as out of control as he was, and he felt her fingernails tear his shoulders. The orgasm was like acid pouring through his body, and he felt her agony, but even within the pain and torment, was pleasure beyond words, beyond comprehension, a pleasure so great it seemed to suck all rationality from his mind.

It blocked every thought except for how much he wanted her, how much he needed her, how fucking amazing it felt to be making love to her, to feel her mind entangled with his, to feel her wet sheath around him, to make love to her again and again and again, to never stop. He could feel her pleasure, pleasure so intense that it hurt, that it was dragging her down into that same spiral of addiction, creating a need neither of them would ever be able to sate. Ever.

A cold fear gripped him even as he drove into her. His willpower was fading. His need to stop, and his need to stay in his own mind were being overcome by the orgasm. It was becoming only about physically connecting with Elisha and immersing himself on who she was. About the pleasure spiraling through both of them. About a pleasure that they could have forever if they didn't fight it.

Dante. Her whisper was a capitulation, a sudden, sensual breath through his mind, no longer fighting the pain, but riding it, living it, wanting it, sucking it into the marrow of her bones until she couldn't live without it, just as he was.

Jesus. It was going to capture them. Forever.

Intense pleasure and satisfaction tore through him, and he almost crowed with the rightness of never ending this moment, of making love to her every second of every day for eternity—

Dante. Forever. I love you.

The words came before he could stop, before he could control them, before he could make himself hold them back. *My Elisha. Forever. I'm yours.*

The night suddenly seemed to scream around them, piercing howls of victory punctuated by a spike in the orgasm that made them both scream. Elisha trembled so violently in his arms that he was afraid she would shatter, and he wrapped his arms even more tightly around her, cradling her in the shield of his body, offering what little strength he still had, trying to help her survive it. It went on and on, an endless circle, until he couldn't hold them up anymore. His legs gave out, and they sank to the ground, still clinging to each other, no longer fighting, no longer screaming, nothing left but each other.

And then, suddenly, it ended again.

Dante collapsed to the earth, cradling Elisha against him as they fell, utterly depleted. He kept her beneath him, using his body as a shield, as if he could protect her from another onslaught. His cock was still hard inside her, and he didn't dare move, not even an inch. They wouldn't survive another round. He was too drained to lift his head, but he did it anyway, needing to see her face, needing to reassure himself that she was all right.

Her eyes were closed, her face pale, her hair drenched with sweat. One hand was still on his shoulder, and the other was on her forehead, as if she was trying to stop the pain. "Elisha?"

Her lashes fluttered, revealing the violet-blue depths. "Dante."

"You all right?"

She shook her head. "No. I'm not all right."

Fear gripped his gut. "Did I hurt you?" He'd been so deep inside her, so rough, and so uncontrolled. "Shit—"

"No, not you. The orgasm is what hurt me." She touched his mouth, silencing him. "You were beautiful."

Her words made something tighten in his chest, something that ached, because he knew she meant it. After what he'd just done to her, she thought he was beautiful. "I'm sorry. I didn't mean to—"

"It's okay." She touched his lips again, and this time, it wasn't to quiet him. It was affection, intimacy, and reassurance. "I'm glad it was you."

He pressed his lips to her fingertips. "Sweetheart, it has to be me. It can't ever be anyone else."

A sad smile played at her mouth. "I know."

"That makes you sad?" The minute he said it, he felt his cock twitch again. She sucked in her breath and gripped his shoulders.

"No, no, no, not again," she whispered. "I can't—"

He braced himself over her, sudden resolve flooding him. "If it happens again, we'll make it through. I have you, Elisha, and I will protect you at all costs. Do you understand? We will be in it together." Desire was plunging through him, ruthless, cruel desire.

Elisha nodded, stiffening beneath him. "Always together," she repeated. "Okay, I'm with you." Her gaze fixed on his. "It doesn't make me sad to be with you," she whispered. "It makes me sad to think that when this is over, when we're torn apart, I will never be in your arms again."

His chest tightened even more, and it became difficult to breathe. "What?" Desire was pounding at him, now, like a relentless din in his head. "Why?" Never in his arms again? Resistance roared through him, a violent rejection of her words.

Her back bowed, and she gasped as the orgasm began to build again. No foreplay. No seduction. Just straight to another orgasm, and he hadn't even moved inside her. "It wasn't just the sex," she gasped. "I meant it. I meant it."

"Meant what?" He gritted his teeth as his body convulsed, as all the muscles in his stomach contracted with such agonizing fierceness he couldn't even move.

"I meant that I loved you. I meant that it's you." She screamed in agony again. "It's only you, Dante. Only you."

He heard her words, he felt them jab his soul. Words that were terrifying, that foretold only terrible things, a fatal future. His brands might not be on her arms, but whatever was between them was even more powerful, consuming, dangerous, and he knew he had to fight it... but he didn't want to.

He simply didn't want to.

He wanted her forever.

He just did.

Somehow, someway, he was going to figure out how to keep her. No matter what.

The moment he had that thought, renewed resolution flooded him, and he looked down at Elisha. Her head was back, her face contorted in a miasma of bliss and agony that sent the deepest, *deepest* need rushing through him. This was his woman, and it was time to save her. With fierce resolve, he braced his hand behind her head, lifting her to him. "Elisha."

She opened her eyes, and those violet-blue depths

fastened onto his. He had no words to explain how he felt. He could not articulate the commitment he'd just made to her, that went deeper than the oath that he'd been compelled to utter by the blood bond. He gave his life to her, right then, forever, but had no words to express the depths of his connection to her. So, he simply smiled at her.

For a moment, her brow furrowed, and then, in the midst of an orgasm threatening to rip them both apart, she smiled back, sealing the connection between them.

In that instant, the orgasm released them. And this time, it was truly gone, whooshing away like a spirit on the wind. He slipped easily from her body, his cock finally spent. With a low groan, he collapsed beside her, immediately dragging her into his arms. Despite the fact she'd been trapped in an orgasm with him that had nearly killed her, she came willingly, burying herself against him as he draped his thigh over her hips and locked his arms around her.

There was nothing left for either of them. Utterly spent, they lay there, together, saying nothing as they held onto each other. Dante knew that the future would come. It would bring choices he did not want to make. It would bring the final stand of the Order, of the queen's darkness, and of the man who had finally capitulated to a woman. All that would come, but in this moment, he didn't care.

In this moment, all that mattered was the woman in his arms.

CHAPTER NINE

The explosion woke them up.

Untangling himself from her with lightning-fast speed, Dante lunged to his feet, his weapons exploding out of his arms in a crack and a flash of black light. Elisha scrambled up, gaping at the top of the mountain. Purple and black plumes were billowing from the top, and red-hot liquid lava was cascading down the side, ripping aside rocks and boulders as it tore across the earth. Towering orange flames yawned toward the sky, tearing apart the fabric of the atmosphere.

Dante moved in front of her, shielding her body with his as he gazed at the mountain. "That's where I have to take the sword, isn't it?"

She sighed. "Yes."

"Into the flames?"

She nodded, watching the flames grow higher. How was he supposed to survive that? She'd had no idea the mountain would erupt like that. She knew her mother was becoming restless, sensing that the sword was closing in on the warrior who would wield it. "Imagine what will happen if the veil is completely severed? That's just the first hint of it."

He looked over at her. "So, I'm supposed to dive into the fire with the sword and sever the veil, then continue onward, and destroy it in the inferno at the base of it?"

She held up her dagger, dangling it from her fingertips as she watched the cascade of color filling the sky. "Want this instead?"

He laughed, sheathing his weapons. "Thanks, but I'll pass. I think we better get Rohan here fast." Dante turned away and quickly gathered their clothes. They both dressed swiftly, neither of them mentioning what had happened when they'd made love, or what it meant. There was no time for discussions about relationships or sex. The end was coming, and it was coming too soon.

Dante gave her hand a quick squeeze that seemed to halt time, and then he turned away, heading back to the rocks he'd arranged in the shape of a pentagram. The symbol stretched across the clearing, the space in the middle large enough to accommodate a grown man. He re-opened the wound on his palm and let a drop of blood land in the very center.

"Do you need mine?"

"No." He glanced at her. "Our blood is mingled now."

At his words, a slow shiver shook her body, and she looked down at her forearm. There was no *sheva* brand visible, but she could still feel Dante's energy swirling through her. Heat cascaded through her body at the memory of what they'd done, how she'd come apart in his arms, and how ruthlessly the orgasm had taken them. She'd said she loved him. *Loved him.* Had she really meant that? A cold chill rippled down her arms as she watched Dante hoist a massive rock and carry it to the center of the pentagram. His muscles were flexed, his shoulders still raw from her fingernails, his jaw grim with determination.

Behind him, the water bubbled and churned in the pool. The water was a seething orange now, flames licking away at the surface of it, and yet Dante did not reach for the sword. Somehow, someway, he was resisting the call, despite the fact it was becoming so strong and compelling. What kind of man could do that? What kind of warrior?

One of honor.

One of conviction.

One of strength beyond comprehension.

He set the boulder down on top of their mingled drop of blood, then braced his palms on it, shifting it to the side a tiny amount, almost infinitesimal. He was so meticulous in his details, a master. No wonder the sword had called him.

She could tell Dante was young, not much more than a hundred years old, and yet there was such a depth to his soul, strength of his character.

He glanced over at her, his palms braced on the rock. "Elisha."

"Yes?"

"Before this shit goes down, I want you to know that I meant what I said." He stood up and walked over to her, his bare feet silent on the arid earth. He brushed her hair back from her face. "I don't know what's going on between us, except that it's dangerous as hell, but I accept that there is an extraordinary connection between us. I will not walk away. We'll figure this sword situation out, and I'll free you from it before it can destroy you. Got it? You're not alone. Never, ever alone again."

At his words, the most incredible warmth flowed through her, and she knew the answer was yes, she'd meant it when she'd told him she loved him. There was so much about him that she didn't know, and yet, he was a part of her soul, a part that had always been there, always waiting to find him. He was why she'd come out of the nether-realm. Somehow, someway, their fate was linked. "Thank you, Dante," she said.

"I'm sorry about what happened. I'm sorry I lost control back there." His eyes were dark, haunted. "I won't touch you again until we figure this out."

"No." She shook her head and took his hand, denying him the right not to touch her. "Don't apologize." She saw the torment in his eyes, and she knew he blamed himself for not being able to control what had happened when they'd made love. She didn't want him to suffer, not when he'd given her so much. "When we made love, it was my choice. The orgasm was driving us, yes, but I still wanted you. And yes, the orgasm was a little over the top, but the physical side was beautiful, the first time it's ever not hurt to be with a man. It's the first time it's ever been my choice. You gave me that gift—"

"What?" His fingers tightened around hers. "You've never had a choice before? It's never been without pain? How many times?"

She didn't want to think about that, not when Dante was with her. She didn't want those memories to intrude. "It doesn't matter—"

"How many times, Elisha? How many times have you had sex without it being your choice?" His voice was low, dark, undulating with rage.

"I don't know. A hundred times? Two hundred?"

Dante's eyes closed. Dark waves of fury rolled off him, so thick that her skin hurt. "Sweet Jesus." He opened his eyes, and went down on one knee before her, taking her hand. "I swear on my Order oath that you will never be without that choice again—"

Before she could answer, the pentagram on the ground began to hum, a violent, lethal sound with an edge that made her skin crawl. Dante spun around, and he went down on one knee again, this time bowing his head as the earth began to churn and spew, dirt and rocks disappearing into the earth as the ground shifted from solid to a seething mass of black smoke.

As she watched, a dark shape began to erupt from the seething smoke. Slowly, it began to rise, as if emerging from the earth itself. A dark hood appeared, a man's head bowed beneath it as the shadowy figure rose further, revealing broad shoulders covered in a cloak that shielded his body from view. His arms were folded across his chest, revealing well-muscled forearms with brands of ancient swords burned onto his flesh. His skin was dark, the color of the earth that had birthed him, and his massive thighs were couched in the thick fur of a dreisen tiger, a legendary creature she'd heard of, but never knew actually existed. But she recognized the patternsin the black fur, and knew that it was.

His calves were bare, his feet almost obscured by the swirling smoke. She could not see his face, hidden beneath the hood, but she felt his eyes burning through her. He was bleeding with raw power, but it was a dark energy, like that of a dangerous predator. It was the power of the nether-realm.

"Elisha," he said, his voice elegant, as if he were a king masquerading as a warrior. "You have come."

She started at his comment. "You know me?"

"You called to me with your blood. There are no secrets now." He turned his head toward Dante, and said nothing, simply waiting.

Dante was still down on one knee, his head bowed.

After a long moment, the warrior she assumed was Rohan swept his cloak to the side and bowed low to Dante. The two warriors held form for a full minute, and then they both rose to their feet again. Rohan stepped out of the smoke and onto the earth. The moment he did so, the earth reformed beneath him, becoming solid again, but the stench of the nether-realm grew heavier.

Instinctively, Elisha slipped her hand into the hidden pocket of her dress, locking her fingers across the Blade of Cormoranth. Rohan was dangerous. While Dante exuded honor and bravery, Rohan carried the taint of death, destruction, and merciless conviction. She knew he was a man never to be trusted. Behind him, the mountain exploded again, spraying lava into the sky that was now burning orange. The pool was boiling fiercely, and she saw that the sword was half out of the water, its handle above the surface now.

They were almost out of time. "Dante," she said fiercely.

"It has to be now."

It was almost impossible to stop himself from taking the sword now. He knew he had only minutes until he succumbed to its power.

Dante fisted his hands as he faced Rohan, every muscle in his body braced against the call of the sword. Images flashed through his mind of the death and destruction he could wreak with it. He could feel the hilt in his palm. He could feel the call of the mountain behind him. "We need your help," he said to Rohan.

Rohan said nothing, but the cold, ruthless touch of his mind was immediate. *Show me.*

Dante opened his mind, and replayed all the events that had transpired, and the future as Elisha had explained it. When he finished, Rohan walked away, turning to face the mountain. "She grows restless," he said. "I can feel her anger. She has become far more powerful than she once was."

"You know her?" Elisha moved up beside Dante, and he instinctively took her hand, urging her to stay behind him. He did not trust Rohan yet, not with her.

"I do." Rohan ran his left hand down his arm, as if caressing his brand. Streaks of blue light crackled along his skin, like lightning bolts leaping from his flesh to his cloak. "Her energy runs strong in you, princess. You carry much darkness, perhaps even more than she."

Elisha glanced at Dante, and her face was pale. "I don't—"

"You are her successor, are you not?" Rohan turned toward her. "You are the future. You are her key to all."

A cold fear settled in Elisha as he spoke words she had long suspected. "I won't let her free," she said.

"It is, my princess, simply a matter of when she is freed. Not if." He lowered his head, as if studying her beneath his hood, and she felt the intensity of his gaze. "You are already in the earth-realm," he said. "You have already begun to free her."

"No." Dante moved in front of her, shielding her with his body. "Elisha is not the enemy, Rohan. It's about the sword. How do we destroy it? Or how do I control it?"

"The child," Rohan said.

"Child?" Elisha repeated. "What child?"

"Your child, princess. Dante's child. The child of the ultimate darkness and the ultimate power."

Elisha stared at him in shock as Dante sucked in his breath. "I can't get pregnant," she said. "Not in the earth-realm. I don't exist here—"

"You will carry his spirit only, guiding him until it is time for him to be born." A faint blue glow emanated from beneath Rohan's hood, illuminating the shadowed outline of a face. She could see a nose, a jaw, black shadows where his eyes were supposed to be. "When it is time, many centuries from now, he will be born to a human woman who will give her life to bring him into this world, to bring your mother's darkest weapon to fruition. He will go by the name Drew, but that is not his true self or his real being."

Elisha was so shocked she didn't know what to say, and Dante's sudden grip on her arm was so tight it almost hurt. "We created a child?" he asked, his voice raw and rough.

"A child destined to destroy all," Rohan answered, "unless we stop him."

"Stop him?" Dante repeated, a low, dangerous tone in his voice. Thick dark violence began to roll off him, cascading through the air. "You mean kill him? Our child? That's what you mean?"

"No!" Elisha was already backing up, covering her belly instinctively, even though he'd said she wasn't carrying the baby physically. "You can't kill him!"

Rohan didn't take his gaze off Elisha. "You have a mission, Dante Sinclair, to protect the world against rogue

Calydons. That is not *my* mission. Mine," he said softly, "is different. Mine is more. Mine can have no mercy." Then there was a boom that shook the earth, and a flash of blue light so bright that she screamed and covered her eyes.

Almost simultaneously, she heard the crack of Dante's weapons and then a piercing pain tore through her. She gasped, clutching her chest as Rohan's sword plunged right into her heart. She stumbled, gasping as her chest glowed with blue light. Vaguely, she heard Dante's outraged bellow, and the roar of weapons clashing, but she couldn't hear anything but the wail of her body as the sword bled its poison into her.

Her legs gave out and she crashed to the ground, gasping as she tried to breathe. She couldn't die. Not yet. It was too soon. She had to stop her mother. And her child. *Her child.* She put her hand to her belly and closed her eyes, fighting to stop the blue from taking her, fighting to hold onto her form. She began to shimmer, her skin sparkled with rainbows, and she knew she was fading, losing her grip on her form.

Instinct screamed at her to hold on, to stay corporeal. Somehow, she knew, *knew*, that if she lost form, the baby would die. She opened her eyes, her gaze foggy as she tried to focus on Dante. He was her anchor. He was her chance. She had to, somehow, connect to his life force. "Dante," she whispered, reaching out for him. *Dante.*

He turned sharply at her call, his dark eyes blazing. *Elisha!* He lunged for her, his hands touching her flesh like the great gift of life. She clutched his hand, fighting to concentrate on his touch, on the sensations that he awakened in her. He made her feel alive, like a woman, like she really existed. Her body responded, flooding back into her physical form, needing to be with him.

Relief rushed through her...and then a yawning emptiness stretched through her as the blue light began to steal her life from the physical body that she'd just anchored herself in. No longer able to fade, she had no escape from the sword that was killing her.

There was no escape. There was no way out. She'd failed on every level, including stopping her mother, and protecting her son. She had failed herself.

Anguished outrage exploded through Dante, a tearing of his very soul as he watched Rohan's sword bury itself in Elisha's heart. "No!" He leapt to his feet and charged Rohan as he unleashed his spears in a quick one-two strike at the man who was his mentor. Rohan blocked the first one, but the second one slammed right into his chest.

Enemy neutralized, Dante sprinted back over to Elisha as Rohan fell to his knees. He scooped her up as she gasped in pain. "Elisha—"

A dark shadow loomed overhead, and Dante looked up as Rohan rose to his feet again, blue light crackling all around him, like lightning unleashed. His hood was still over his face, blocking it, but Dante felt his gaze bearing down on them. His ruthless intent coated the night like a blanket of death.

His spear could not seriously harm Rohan any more than Rohan's sword could have harmed Dante. They were both too immortal, too powerful, and too strong.

Rohan swung toward him, his cloak sweeping out as he raised his sword. Blue light crackled down the blade, as if it were alive. "No!" Dante set Elisha aside and lunged to his feet. "Come to me," he shouted into the night, at the sword he'd been denying for so long. "Come to me now!"

It exploded from the pool and hurtled through the air at him, water streaming off the blade. It slammed into his palm. The power that surged through him was instant, explosive, and he screamed with the intensity of it. This time, he didn't try to contain it or shield himself from it. He embraced it, drinking it into himself as he whirled toward Rohan, who had frozen, his sword pointing at Elisha's throat.

"Back off," Dante growled, his voice lower and darker than it had ever been. "Don't touch her."

Rohan went still, turning his sword to Dante. "Drop the sword, Dante," he said in a low voice. "Drop it while you can."

"It's too late." Fierce dark anger swirled through him, power so intense it seemed to bleed from his pores as he circled toward Elisha, who was still gasping on the ground. "Save her life, you bastard."

"No." Rohan turned with him, his sword out and ready. But he didn't strike, and Dante knew it was because he had no chance against the sword Dante held.

"Yes, or you die."

Rohan growled. "I accept death."

"Do you?" Dante knelt beside Elisha, and his heart nearly stopped at the pain in her eyes. Suddenly, it didn't matter about the child that he didn't even know. He just wanted *her*. Her skin was glowing blue, poisoned by Rohan's sword. Only Rohan could save her from what he'd done to her. "If you die, Rohan, you get to save no one, ever again. If you let her live, then you can try to kill our child another day."

Rohan swore, his blade still out. "I accept death," he said again.

Keeping his sword free, Dante picked up Elisha again, cradling her against his chest. "Do you? What if you die? Who will fulfill your mission? No one. You're the last one of your kind, and I *will* kill you to save her." He let his intention fill his mind, opening his thoughts to the other Calydon, letting Rohan see what he meant.

"Your protective runes still glow, but you hold her as if she is your *sheva*," Rohan said, still moving slowly around them, his sword still out, no doubt looking for an opening. "You do not think clearly."

"I think you're the one not thinking clearly." Elisha coughed, and urgency coursed through Dante. "Don't you get it?" he shouted. "I'll kill you, and then you can't save anyone else!

Is that your mission? To die and leave the earth unprotected? Is it? Save her and help us close the veil! There's time to stop her later!" But even as he spoke, the sword burned in his palm, and his skin began to smoke. Dark, fierce resolution tore through him, along with the need to open that veil, to release all that it held back. Swearing, he looked at Rohan. "Do you feel what's going through me? What is it, great seer? What the fuck do I feel?"

Rohan's energy pulsed at him, and then he swore. "The woman is all that keeps the sword from consuming you completely."

"If she dies, it takes me. And if it takes me, I'm going to open that veil and let all that shit into our world." Dante clutched Elisha closer, fighting the images in his head of the veil opening, of a massive dark shadow streaking out of the volcano, of darkness descending upon them all. "And then, you will have failed in the only thing that matters to you, because you won't be able to stop me, not when I'm using this sword, and you know it. Your *only* chance is to work with us, not against us."

For a long moment, Rohan did not move, and then with a sound like air being sucked into a vacuum, he sheathed his weapons. "Bring her to me."

Satisfaction burned through Dante as he sprinted toward the other Calydon. They both went down on their knees as they came together, and Rohan placed his hands over Elisha's chest.

His hands glowed a golden color, and he nodded at Dante. Together, they chanted the words that he'd trusted Dante with so long ago, when Rohan had needed Dante's help to save the one person who had mattered to him. Words so powerful that the earth shuddered beneath them, words that were powerless if chanted alone, words that gained their power from the sharing of spirits, powerful spirits, warrior spirits. Rohan was the last of his kind, and Dante was the only one he'd found powerful enough to assist in the chant.

Together, they fought for Elisha. Together, they battled for the chance to defeat the sword.

Rohan's hands glowed even brighter, as they continued the chant.

Dante waited for the first flecks of blue to appear on Rohan's hands, but they didn't. His palms simply stayed gold. Elisha sagged against his chest, her body now streaked with black shadows among the blue. "What's wrong? Why isn't it working?"

Rohan shook his head. "She's too powerful in her own right. I can't override it. We need more strength. We need more than we can generate."

"Shit!" Dante focused harder, chanting more loudly, and he felt Rohan do the same. The other Calydon's urgency was obvious, as he apparently now understood the immediate cost if Elisha died, but Dante had nothing to ground him.

"We need more," Rohan said. "Where is Louis? The Calydon you were hunting?"

Dante didn't bother to ask how Rohan knew he'd been after Louis. "Dead." But even as he said the words, he thought of the young Calydon who had tried to join him, the one brimming with such anger and fire. Hope rushed through him and he immediately reached out with his mind, seeking to connect with the younger warrior. *Zach. It's your time. Come. Now.*

There was a sudden burst of white-hot energy in his mind, a searing flash of anguish so penetrating it was like his soul had been ripped into fragments. Zach's suffering was so extreme, so debilitating that Dante stopped in shock. Never had he felt such despair and grief from another Calydon, except from Rohan when they'd first met. Rohan, who was deadly, unpredictable, and the only warrior Dante trusted.

His father would have killed Zach instantly, slitting his throat rather than allowing such emotion to bleed into the earth, but that emotion, that pain, that grief...it was the power Dante needed. It was the power that none of the prior Order members had possessed. It was the power of the soul. *Zach!* He thrust his energy toward the younger warrior, fierce and relentless. *Look at this woman!* He focused his gaze on Elisha, and his own gut wrenched when he saw her so limp in his arms. Her skin was ashen, blood trickling from the corner of her mouth. Jesus. She was dying. Anguish tore through him, and this time, it wasn't Zach's. It was his own.

Grimly, knowing it was the only way to reach the warrior who could save her, Dante accepted his own grief and shared it with Zach. *She's dying, Zach, and we can't save her without your help. She's an innocent.*

There was a strangled bellow of grief from Zach, and Dante saw the images flash through his mind of the family that had been murdered only hours ago. Zach's family. *Get the fuck out of my head!*

I need you! Dante held Elisha tighter, letting Zach feel his pain, forcing the younger warrior to feel the gradual fade of her spirit. *You couldn't save those you love, but you can save this woman. Are you really going to let her die?*

Another crash of despair so agonizing that Dante had to shield himself from it to keep from collapsing. *Zach.* He sent a push at the other warrior, a command. *You survived for a reason, Zach. You owe it to your family to save others. With each life you save, you honor their death. Get up, pull yourself together, and get your ass over here. Now. Or Elisha's death will be on your shoulders far more than your family's. You were not able to save them, but at least you tried. If you don't try now, then it's a violation of your family's belief in you. Come. Now.*

He sent the last word as an unyielding order, calling upon the guilt, anguish, and other emotions that his father would have deemed an unforgivable weakness. He called upon them, using them to galvanize the kind of response that could only be driven by a warrior who was truly alive in his soul.

Tormented, yes, but alive.

For a moment, he felt only Zach's pulsating grief and guilt. Then suddenly, there was a surge of fury. *I'm coming.* In the distance, in the direction of the village, there was a sudden explosion, flames reaching up as high as the trees, a ball of fire that exploded through the night, streaking through the woods at unbelievable speed.

Satisfaction pulsed through Dante as he looked back at Rohan. "He's on his way."

Rohan was watching the fire searing the night. "He needs to learn to control that," he observed. "But there is much power within him. More than he knows."

"I agree."

Dante watched as the fireball rolled toward them, burning through the vegetation. So much anger in the kid, and so much emotion. Too much, in fact. The youth was out of control, unable to contain his energy. He was violent and wild, with no discipline. He had no chance to become Order, to be the warrior that Dante needed him to be.

But he was also their only hope.

CHAPTER TEN

Zach arrived in a raging fireball of orange and red flames. It exploded around them with a loud crack, showering the clearing with sparks that sizzled and hissed on the dry ground. Dante swore and covered Elisha with his body, letting the sparks hit his back instead of her. "Take it down," he yelled at Zach. "You're going to start a forest fire!"

Zach stumbled as the fireball released him, his knees bloodied and raw as he fought for balance. He glanced vaguely around the clearing, as if trying to comprehend what Dante had just said. Dante swore, shocked by how far Zach had sunk in just the few hours since he'd lost his family to Louis. The warrior was bruised and battered, all his wounds as open and raw as they'd been before. He hadn't healed himself at all.

Zach's body was streaked with blood, and his eyes were empty pits of grief so deep that it had turned his face into sunken gray shadows. For a split second, Dante felt pity for him, for the grief and anguish that could strip a man of all he was in a matter of hours. Zach's head swiveled around, and his gaze finally fell upon Dante. His eyes seemed to focus, and he shook his head, as if to clear it. "What?"

Dante realized how out-of-control Zach had allowed himself to become, and he began to doubt whether Zach would be able to focus enough to help them. Shit. Zach was their only chance! He had to bring the kid back. "Your sparks are burning up the clearing," he said, keeping his voice calm and focused, as he continued to hold Elisha, counting the seconds between each of her breaths, knowing that they were almost out of time. "Fix it."

Zach swung his head around to look. He seemed barely able to comprehend it, but he finally raised his left hand. There was a loud, violent burst of energy, and then the flames died out, sputtering and angry, as if they were bitter that their master had sucked their lives from them. Zach turned back to Dante, his shoulders hunched and bent. Dante saw he'd marked himself with ancient designs across his chest, the signs of honoring a dead loved one. Zach had used symbols Dante was sure hadn't been used in centuries, symbols dating back to the days before the Order even existed. How had the younger warrior even learned about them?

For a split second, he wondered if there was more to Zach than he'd first sensed...but he had no time for that. Not now. "To your knees," he commanded.

Flames appeared to be flickering weakly in the younger warrior's dark eyes as he looked down and saw Elisha. For a split second, he stared blankly at her, then sudden fury exploded from him in a surge of black smoke, and his eyes seemed to ignite. "Who hurt her?" he snapped as he dropped to his knees beside her. "What fucking hurt her?" His voice was laced with that same, unchained fury that Dante had seen earlier. So much anger and emotion in him. Too much. Shit. Dante's instinct was to shut the kid down, but that was what they needed right now. Power.

"Stay focused and use your energy to heal her," Dante said instead, willing a calming energy toward Zach. "We need to save her. Follow our lead."

Zach looked sharply at Dante, and then he nodded, keeping his gaze fixed on Dante, as if he could sense the control that Dante was offering him. Flames seemed to shimmer beneath his skin, but he didn't ignite, somehow containing the fire that raged within him.

"Now." Again, Rohan set his hands on Elisha's chest, his palms glowing gold almost immediately. Dante resumed his position, and Zach mimicked his stance. As Rohan began to chant again, Dante joined in. For a moment, Zach merely watched Dante intently, boldly probing Dante's mind for the words. Dante resisted the urge to shut him out, and instead showed Zach what he wanted him to do. Zach immediately joined in the chant, his deep voice vibrating with more power and strength than Dante had even hoped for.

The rush of energy flooded them, and Rohan nodded at Dante, both of them realizing that they had vastly underestimated the magnitude of Zach's power. Together, they summoned their healing energy, the rhythmic chant rising in crescendo, Zach echoing them. The power of the trio rose and streaked through them, like a fierce, dark force crushing them, bearing down on their flesh with more and more pressure. For a long, agonizing moment, Rohan's hands stayed gold, the power not transferring to Elisha. Panic hammered at Dante. "Elisha!" He shouted her name and thrust every last bit of power he had into her. "Come back to me!"

Suddenly, there were streaks of blue light across his knuckles. Rohan whooped, and relief rushed through Dante as he watched the first streaks of gold begin to flash over Elisha's skin, signaling that the energy was beginning to shift between Rohan and Elisha: his poison returning to him, and his healing light penetrating her. Son of a bitch. Zach's added strength had made the difference.

Dante grinned at Zach. *Thank you.*

Did you kill her? Because I'm still going to kill whoever hurt her. Zach didn't look up, and he didn't even pause in his fierce chant, but his skin began to flicker even more.

Dante watched him grimly, knowing the warrior was a breath away from exploding and destroying everything around him, the mark of a liability, not an asset. Instinctively, he moved his shoulder in front of Zach, blocking Elisha from him as the three of them continued to chant. Dante reached out with his mind to his woman, searching for a response, but her mind was quiet, not answering. *Elisha. Come back to me. I need you.* He couldn't keep the urgency out of his voice, the rising tension as the sword pulsed more fiercely at him. He could feel the mountain's pressure building, summoning him and the sword to the peak. Swearing, Dante buried his face in her hair, fighting desperately against the summons. He would not leave her. *He would not leave her.*

Rohan's voice rose, and the night grew brighter. His golden light filled the air as he swiftly stripped the blue light from Elisha. It flooded his body and spilled over into Dante, who had already steeled himself for the assault. "Watch it," he warned Zach belatedly...too late.

The younger warrior sucked in his breath and his body went rigid, fighting against the brutal sensation of pain that Dante knew he was feeling. The first time he'd felt Rohan's energy it had nearly killed him. *Come on, Zach. Stay with us.*

Zach looked at him, fierce determination on his face as sudden flames erupted from his body. Dante swore at the heat and leaned forward, using his upper body to shield Elisha from the fire. *What the fuck are you doing?*

Staying alive. That shit's powerful. I need to burn it up.

Chant! Rohan's command broke through the moment, and both Calydons focused on it, the three deep voices joining together in the ancient ritual melody. As he chanted, Dante sent his own healing energy into Elisha. It would not help with Rohan's curse, but he had to shield her from Zach's fire, which was glowing even brighter. The flames had not burned Zach, but they were hot enough to incinerate the rest of them. Pain burned his flesh, and he saw Elisha's skin darken as well. "Hurry," Dante shouted at Rohan.

Rohan said nothing, but there was another burst of

power from him, and the blue and golden light began to crackle like a dozen lightning bolts slamming down around them. Zach's flames grew higher. Elisha's skin shifted from blue to gold. The blue that had been stripped from her body coursed through them all as the warriors jointly took it from her. Dante's skin began to blister from Zach's flames, and the sword burned his hand, urging him to use it against Zach and stop him before he could burn them all up. Dante gritted his teeth and held Elisha tighter against him, focusing only on her, on her spirit, on her strength, on their connection, knowing that she was all that stood between him and the lethal future that the sword was guiding him inexorably toward.

Dante's presence burst into her mind with sudden warmth. Elisha gasped, then coughed as air rushed back into her body.

"Elisha." His voice seemed to fill her with life, with energy, with strength, and she opened her eyes.

Dante was leaning over her, his face gaunt with concern, even as he smiled. "Welcome back, sweetheart."

She touched his face, needing to know that it was real, that somehow, someway, he'd pulled her back. His skin was warm and rough, his whiskers prickling her fingers. "Dante? I thought I was dead."

His smile faded. "You were close." His arms tightened around her, and she became aware that she was on his lap, wrapped in his embrace. "How do you feel?"

"I'm okay." Her body ached, and she felt weak, but definitely alive. "What happened?" But even as she asked the question, she remembered Rohan's sword plunging into her chest. Instinctively, she grabbed for her chest, but there was no sword there. Not even a mark. "Did Roha—"

Then she saw him, kneeling beside Dante. Fear tore through her and she lunged to her feet, scrambling to get the

Blade of Cormoranth from the folds of her dress. She held up the knife, backing away, her heart pounding. Her breath was wheezing in her chest, and her legs were still dangerously weak. "You killed me!" Behind him stood another warrior who had stepped back, orange and red flames cascading from his body and dancing in the night air.

"Hey." Dante stood up quickly, moving between her and the others as he slipped his arm around her waist, holding her up. "It's okay, Elisha. They're on our side."

"He killed me." She didn't take her gaze off Rohan, who was still down on one knee. His hood was still covering his face, but his head was turned at such an angle that she knew he was watching her. Dark energy was surging around him, like a deadly smoke that was oozing from his pores. But it wasn't smoke. It was a mist that was almost alive...

"Yeah, but then he saved your life. In guy speak, that means we're good." Dante squeezed her around the waist. "Don't kill him yet, sweetheart. We need his help. We need both their help. Kill him later, okay?"

His voice was so strained and tense that it wrenched her from her panic. She looked sharply at him, her arm already trembling with fatigue from holding the blade. "What's wrong?" Her heart was pounding now in fear for her life, fear for Dante, and fear of everything spinning out of control around her. She felt like her brain was still foggy, and she couldn't clear her thoughts. "Are you okay?"

In answer, he raised his hand. Clenched in his fist was the sword from the queen's darkness. His knuckles were already black with taint. His hand was trembling slightly, and the tendons in his forearms were so taut they strained against his skin.

Cold terror seemed to plunge into her bones. "Oh my God. Dante!" She put her hand over his, and felt the cold bite of her world. "Put it down!"

"I can't." His voice was grim. "I can't get my hand off it."

She looked more closely, and saw that his skin had fused to the hilt, becoming a part of it. "Oh, no." She spun around to look at the mountain, and saw that the flames were billowing up to the heavens, and streams of lava were cascading down the side of the mountain. There weren't even any footpaths left to climb. The path to the top of the mountain was directly through the deadly heat and fire. "It's too late." She gripped his arm, staring at the mountain as anguish filled her. "We've lost our chance. There's no way to get into the mountain alive anymore. The lava will kill you." Tears burned in her eyes, and her throat tightened with anguish as she held onto him, terrified to let him go. "The sword will take your body to the inferno within and sever the veil. You won't survive long enough to redirect it." How could it have gotten to this point? How could Dante die? How could this be happening?

Someone moved behind her, and she spun back to Rohan, who had risen to his feet. Despite Dante's claim, she could feel the darkness of his soul, and she stepped backward, holding the dagger higher. "We don't have time for this," she shouted at him. "Dante's your friend! We need your help! Don't you feel anything toward the man who helped keep you alive through a century of hell?"

Rohan went still. "I feel enough," he said, his voice like the edge of a cold knife cutting across her mind.

"Do you? Then help us!" She ignored Dante's restraining hand on her arm. It was just too much to deal with, the idea of losing him, of losing it all, of failing on so many levels. "Just help us!"

"Wait a second." The fiery warrior hadn't moved, though the fire on his flesh had thickened, raging off him. On his arms were the black Calydon brands in the shape of an ancient sai. His eyes were glittering with anger. "*Who* tried to kill you?" he asked her, his voice low with fury, laced with deadly intent. "*Who* was it that almost killed an innocent? A woman?"

Chills rippled down her arms at the intensity of his

expression, and the rawness of his face. There was so much anguish and torment in his eyes that his entire body was trembling. "I—" She paused in her answer, suddenly unsure what the truth would unleash from this warrior. Her gaze slid inadvertently to Rohan, then back to the younger warrior. "Why?"

"It really was him?" Zach spun toward Rohan, and a fireball appeared in his hand. Rage flared in his eyes, outrage that seemed to scream through the night as he reared back to whip it at Rohan. "You bastard! You killed an innocent—"

Rohan pointed his index finger at Zach. Blue light exploded from his finger and smacked Zach in the chest. The warrior flew backward and crashed into a tree. "Shut up." He turned back to Elisha, ignoring the younger warrior's groan of pain.

"What is wrong with you?" Elisha snapped at Rohan as she started to run toward the downed warrior, but Rohan caught her arm and jerked her back.

"The queen's darkness must be stopped," he said, his voice biting and relentless. "Dante must destroy the sword. It is the only way."

"Let her go." Dante jumped between them, the sword of the queen's darkness pointed at Rohan's neck. "Don't touch her."

Elisha's heart began to thunder at the raw intensity of Dante's voice. His body was rigid and tense, his eyes blazing with anger that was on the edge of taking him. "Dante," she said softly, fighting to keep the panic out of her voice. "It's the sword, turning you against him—"

"No. It's the fact he's hurting you, and he won't back off." He glanced at her. "You come before the veil, Elisha. Always."

Her heart softened at his words, at his commitment. "Aren't you supposed to be a warrior?"

"Yeah. I'm your warrior." And with those words, he wrapped his free hand around hers and turned to face Rohan, his sword still at the other warrior's neck. "But I'd sure like to save the world, too."

She was too tired to fight him anymore, too exhausted to play the martyr and tell him to let her die. She didn't want either of them to die. She wanted it all to work out, somehow, someway. "Rohan," she whispered. "Help us." She knew that the darkness of the nether-realm flowed strongly through him, strong enough that he might indeed have a way to help them, if he chose.

For a long moment, none of them moved, then finally Rohan released her arm and held up his hand in a silent statement that he would not try to hurt her for now. "Those runes are barely working," Rohan said softly. "They're not going to hold." His gaze went between them. "The pull between the two of you is too strong. You're going to trigger the *sheva* fate."

"It will hold." Dante lowered the sword from Rohan's neck, but kept it pointed at him. "If I destroy the sword, Elisha will die. How do we stop that?"

"There's no way to stop it, Dante. You'll die the minute the flames take you. You won't be able to destroy it." Elisha's fingers tightened around the Blade of Cormoranth as the truth hit her. If Dante had no chance of destroying the sword, then she couldn't let him go in there. She looked down at the blade, and shook her head. How could she kill him? How could she stop him? "There's no way you'll survive the fire long enough to make any choices, even if there are any," she whispered. "Rohan doesn't matter."

"No? I say there's a way." Dante looked past her, still clasping her hand. "Zach," he said to the warrior who was still sprawled on the ground, his hand pressed to a blue, glowing gash on his chest. "Can you protect me against the fire? Create a shield to allow me to climb up there?"

"Us," Elisha corrected, her heart leaping with sudden adrenaline. Was there really hope? Between all of them, could they do it? "You need me. You'll never find the inferno on your own."

Dante glared at her. "I won't endanger you—"

"It's not your choice. I care about this world, too." She looked at Zach, at the fire still pouring from his body. "Can you do it? Can you help?"

He looked at the mountain, and for a brief second his eyes seemed to glow red, reflecting the flames. "If I don't, what happens?"

"The queen's darkness will be unleashed into the world, and then will infect it with its poison." Dante said. "It will destroy this realm."

"And curse it," Rohan added.

Zach's face darkened with the anger she'd seen earlier. "And innocents will die?" He asked the question of her, as if he didn't trust the men.

"All of them," she whispered.

Soul-deep pain flashed across his face. "Fuck that." Still crumpled on the ground from Rohan's attack, sudden energy seemed to leap through him. "You tell me what you need, and I'll make it happen." He surged to his feet, staggering slightly. "No more death," he growled. "No more innocents die. *Ever.*" Fire began to lick at the ends of his hair, flickering violently.

Dante looked at Rohan, his jaw tight with determination. "We can get in. How do we protect Elisha from dying when I destroy the sword?"

Rohan looked back and forth between them. "After you sever the veil, I will hold it together to give you time to destroy the sword."

Elisha frowned at him. Yes, she knew that he carried with him some of the energy of the nether-realm, but holding the veil together was different. "That's impossible. No one can do that—"

Rohan swung his head to look at her. Slowly, he raised his right hand. Crackles of blue electricity seemed to leap across his palm. He reared back and hurled the light at the burning mountain. The light hit the peak, and an eerie wail cut through the night, as the mountain screamed its pain. The lava turned blue for a split second, before reverting back to orange and red. "It is what I do, princess."

And then she knew. She could hear it in his voice. Even if there was a way, he was not going to save her life when Dante destroyed the sword. He didn't want her to live. He would hold the veil closed to protect his earth, but he would not save her life.

Dante swore and caught her arm, apparently drawing the same conclusion. "There has to be a way to save her," he said. "What is it? You know all about the nether-realm and the queen's realm. *What is the key?*"

Rohan's head bowed, as if he were looking at Dante's cursed foot, then slowly he raised his head again. "There is no key," he said quietly. "The choice must be made. Sacrifice one innocent for the greater good, or save one innocent at the cost of all others." His gaze seemed to bore into Dante. "Will you sacrifice one innocent to save the others? Act for the greater good? That is your father's legacy, Dante, his words, the mission of the Order of the Blade as it was meant to be. Will you fulfill your birthright, or will you save one woman and destroy the earth?"

Chapter Eleven

Dante's skin went cold at Rohan's challenge. It was a brutal cold that went right to the marrow of his bones. Sacrifice Elisha to save others? Sacrifice the world to save her? Neither was okay. Neither option was acceptable. "No," he said. "*No! There has to be another way—*"

The mountain exploded with another loud roar, and suddenly his hand burned with fire. A fierce, raw rush of power flooded him, and he involuntarily turned toward the mountain. Fire tumbled toward him, catapulting down the rocky sides. The sword began to pull at him, dragging him toward the fire. Unable to stop himself, he took a step toward the peak. Then another step. Swearing, he dug his feet into the earth, but his head was pounding with visions of death, destruction, and power. He went down to his knees, struggling to resist the pull, his body screaming with the effort of fighting the summons.

Elisha knelt in front of him, clasping his face with her hands. "Dante, look at me."

"Elisha," he croaked, searching her face. He saw the haunted depths in her eyes, the love shimmering on her face, and he knew the truth. He was not the man he needed to be to make this right. He had to spare them all the burden of who he was. "Use the dagger," he gasped. "Use it on me now. I won't let myself destroy you."

Tears filled her eyes. "You would die rather than save the world?"

"I won't be my father," he gritted out. "Innocents won't be sacrificed." With his free hand, he slid his fingers through her hair, pulling her so his forehead was against hers. "One life is never less worthy than the other. I can't sacrifice you—"

"If you choose for me to live," she said, her body shaking, "then you have made the choice of sacrificing millions of innocents to save one. Either way, you have to sacrifice someone."

"No!" Anguish tore through him, and he gripped her more tightly. "You can't die!"

Tears were streaming down her cheeks. "If I use the dagger on your successor, it will eventually kill me. I will no longer be here to protect the sword. I die either way, Dante, but if you fight for this, if you destroy the sword now, then it can end. Then my death is not in vain."

"Fuck!" Denial raged through him, anger and outrage that his father had won, that his father would still have a son who would take an innocent life for a greater purpose. "I can't do this—"

"You are not him," she whispered, holding his face, her violet-blue eyes searching his. "He killed for his own pleasure. For his own power. He sacrificed innocents, but not for a noble purpose or the true greater good. *You are not him,* Dante." She placed her hand over his heart. "You are good and pure, and your choice is beautiful. You must do it, and you know it, but it will never, *ever*, make you your father."

Dante locked his hand behind her head and dragged her to him, slamming his mouth over hers. He needed to kiss her, to hold her, to lose himself in her one last time. She was right. He knew she was. Sacrifice millions just to save one woman would be the selfish choice his father would have made. But to let her die... His throat tightened and he pulled back. "I love you," he said hoarsely. "I love you, Elisha. With all that is left of my soul, whatever that is."

She smiled. "I know you do, Dante."

"We must go," Rohan interrupted, his voice tense with urgency. "It is time."

Dante looked up at the warrior who had helped him survive so much. "What about our child? What will happen to him if Elisha dies now? If I die? Does his spirit have enough of a grip in this realm to survive without us?"

"No. Not by himself."

Jesus. His child would die, too? A new wave of grief seemed to consume him. He looked at Elisha, and tears were streaming down her face, tears blackened with the soot that was drifting down from the mountaintop. She swallowed, then spoke, her voice trembling. "I'm not carrying him in my body," she said. "If he needs us, then it's only on a spiritual level. Since he came from both of us, either one of us surviving will be enough. He doesn't need me. Just you." She held his face, her hands shaking. "You must survive, Dante. You're the only one who has a chance!"

Dante shook his head, memories of his own mother dying flashing through his mind. "He will not grow up without a mother—"

"I have to die," she interrupted. "You don't!"

"What about my foot? Aren't I dying, too?"

They both looked down, and he saw that the curse had been working its way up his leg. His calf was twisted and mangled, and his knee was turning black. "I'm dying, too, Elisha."

She gripped his arm in sheer terror. "One of us must find a way," she whispered urgently, her voice thick with tears. "One of us must! For him!"

He had a sudden vision of Elisha dying, of their son fading into nothing before he was even born, and anguish ripped through him. Dante wrapped his arm around her and crushed her against him, fighting against the sudden pain in his chest. Pain so intense that it felt like a thousand knives were carving his heart out of his body. This was what his father had warned against. This kind of pain. This kind of emotion. It made a man weak. Vulnerable. It would force him to make the wrong choices, choices based on his heart instead of his mind. He needed to be the steely warrior, to hide the pain, to focus, to clear his mind so he could see his path. He fought it back, struggled to contain it, but it wouldn't leave. He couldn't get the pain out of his chest. He couldn't rid his mind of the visions of Elisha and his son dying—

There was a sudden scream, and Elisha was ripped from his arms. He opened his eyes to see her being dragged backward toward the mountain, her fingers cleaving claw marks into the parched earth. She screamed his name, her eyes wide with fear as she was torn away from him.

"Elisha!" He lunged to his feet and raced after her, but the faster he went, the faster she seemed to go, staying just out of his reach. "Elisha!" he bellowed.

"The call of the queen's darkness is too strong," Rohan said as he caught up, running hard beside Dante. "It's summoning the sword, but since Elisha is from the same realm, it's taking her as well. It's calling back everything from that realm."

"Well, fuck that!" Summoning all his strength, Dante lunged for her and caught her wrist. The moment his fingers closed around hers, he was dragged off his feet, tumbling over the rocky terrain as the sword dragged them both up the mountain toward the raging fire.

Elisha's fingers wrapped around his, and she met his gaze as he righted himself, fighting for footing. His bare feet sliced over the rocks, and he swore as his cursed foot smashed into a sharp boulder. Ahead of them, the towering wall of fire got closer and closer, until the air was so hot that his flesh burned. He glanced over his shoulder, and saw that Zach and Rohan were far behind, unable to keep pace with the pull of the darkness dragging them forward. "Zach!" he bellowed. "Get your ass up here!"

Elisha's feet touched the fire, and she screamed in pain.

There was a roar of outrage behind them, and suddenly a massive black and orange fireball tore past them and exploded around them. The flames of darkness shrieked in outrage and drew back, opening a path for them. Another human-sized fireball rolled past them and then exploded just in front of them, disgorging Rohan and Zach into the fiery inferno.

Zach spun around and thrust his palms into the air. "This is for my family," he bellowed, his voice reverberating through the raging din. Fire exploded from him, springing up in violent rages all around them until the four of them were encased in a raging bubble of safety, as Zach's flames built a protective wall between them and the assault from the queen's darkness. The pull of the mountain suddenly ceased, unable to penetrate the wall of fire that Zach had built around them.

"Shit," Rohan stared at him. "I didn't think you could do it. That's impressive as hell."

Flames were dancing in Zach's eyes. "For my family," he repeated. "No one else dies." His words were thick with anguish and grief, twisted by the deaths of those he loved. The agonizing emotions were giving him power beyond what he should have been able to do.

Zach was not a cold, reserved, stoic warrior like Dante's father had recruited for the Order. He was damaged, exhausted, grieving, and full of hate for those who had stolen what mattered to him...and that had made him powerful enough to hold off the queen's darkness.

Had Dante's father been wrong? Were the warriors the Order needed actually the fucked-up, damaged men who had suffered so much loss that they bled their suffering into their every move? Was that what it took to resist the allure of power and be immune to corruption? Was the secret to be driven by a past so terrible that nothing else mattered but surviving and fixing that nightmare?

Dante looked at Elisha, who had fallen to her knees, gasping for air. Her face was covered in soot, her hair singed on the ends, and her fingers still clenched around the hilt of her dagger. Fierce protectiveness surged through him. Was she his answer? Was she what would give him strength, like Zach's family had done for him? Was he supposed to feel the grief of losing her and let it consume him? Or was his father right? Did he need to stay logical and focused in battle? Which was it? *Which was it?*

The flames around them rose higher, and Dante felt the mountain begin to call him again, a fierce, pulsating summons.

"I can't hold it much longer," Zach shouted. "We gotta keep moving!"

Elisha was dragged a few yards across the ground, her fingers gripping the dirt as the queen's darkness began to call her again. She looked up at him. "Find a way to live," she said. "You must!"

"Elisha!" Dante lunged for her, but his fingers closed on empty air as she was ripped off the ground and yanked through the wall of flames, disappearing from sight.

There was no longer a choice to be made. There were no longer multiple options. There was no longer the opportunity for a clear, concise strategy. The moment Dante saw Elisha sucked into the vortex of darkness, his entire soul screamed for her, and all that mattered was getting her back.

"Elisha!" he bellowed as he lurched to his feet. "Take me, you bastard," he shouted to the sword. "Take me!" And with that, he dropped all his resistance to the weapon. The moment he stopped fighting it, its power swarmed through him, like a violent poison slicing away at his very soul. His will seemed to be sucked out of him, replaced by a compulsion to accede to the call of the sword.

Dark purpose swarmed him. The veil. *The veil.* He had to open it. *Now!*

"Hold on to me!" He commanded Rohan and Zach as he was ripped off his feet by the sword. It sped toward the peak of the mountain, dragging him ruthlessly toward where Elisha had vanished. Elisha. *Elisha.* He focused all his attention on the image of her eyes, on her scent, on the sensation of her body against his, using her as an anchor to keep his sanity from being consumed by the sword. As he did, he became gradually aware of Rohan and Zach gripping his arm, being dragged along with him. Zach continued to spew flames, clearing a path so they weren't all incinerated by the fire.

"Elisha!" he yelled over the flames at Zach. "Help her!"

In response, Zach hurled another massive fireball ahead of them. It exploded somewhere in the distance, and Dante could only hope that it had given her respite. Again and again, Zach threw fireballs. At the same time, he kept their shield burning around them. Despite his efforts, it was still getting hotter and hotter, and the flames seemed to be closing in on them, mingling with Zach's protections.

The sword was burning his palm, vibrating so violently it felt as if his arm was going to be torn from his side. "We're getting close," he yelled.

And then he saw it. Up ahead was a shimmering, iridescent, almost translucent sphere. Sprawled across the surface of it was Elisha. She was alive and unburned! Relief rushed through him for a split second, until he realized her body was shaking violently as the queen's darkness tried to drag her through the veil, but couldn't. "Elisha!" There was another burst of energy from the sword, and then it was dragging him straight down toward her, the point of it directed right at the veil she was lying on, ready to slice it open.

Swearing, he tried to divert it so he wouldn't pierce the veil, but the sword was too strong. He couldn't fight it. "Rohan, get ready!"

"I'm on it!" Rohan shouted back.

He suddenly noticed the point of the sword was heading directly for Elisha. He realized the call was at its strongest at that place, pulling both the sword and Elisha to the same spot. "Elisha!" he bellowed. "Move!" He wrenched violently at the sword with both hands, but he couldn't redirect it. He had no control. None! He was getting closer and closer, heading directly toward her heart. "Elisha! Wake up!"

Her eyes fluttered open, and her blue-violet gaze swiveled weakly toward him. She didn't look at the sword. She just looked at him.

He realized she was too weak to speak, let alone move.

Jesus. He was going to kill her. The sword was going to go right through her in order to get to the veil! "Elisha!" Outrage and terror spewed through him, along with a fear so deep it seemed to cleave his soul in half. Almost in slow motion, he watched the tip of the sword plunge toward her. He heard Zach's howl of outrage. He felt Rohan reaching past him, ready to grip the veil and hold it together. He heard his own bellow of denial. But all he could see was the face of the woman he loved, the mother of his son, the woman so brave she was willing to die for the cause she believed in.

Weakly, she lifted her hand, reaching toward him, as if she were silently imploring him for... mercy? Love? Strength? Was he that weak that he couldn't save her? Was he the pathetic underachiever his father had tried to murder in disgust? *No.* "No!" With a roar of fury, Dante ripped his hand free of the hilt, grabbed the sword with both hands, and dragged himself along the length of the blade, closer and closer to the tip, even as it streaked toward Elisha, until it was almost there—

He threw himself in front of the tip of the blade, knocking her body out of the way just as the sword struck. It went right though his chest and into the veil. The pain was so violent, so extreme that his mouth opened in wordless, silent agony, his very breath sucked from him. His body spasmed and then went rigid, cursed by the blackness of all that the sword contained.

There was an earsplitting shriek as the veil ripped apart. Elisha tumbled through the opening and Dante fell after her. As they fell, he managed to look up just as blue electricity crackled across the veil, weaving it back together. It bucked and surged against Rohan's defense, and Dante knew it wouldn't hold for long.

They tumbled through the air, buffeted by black mist and thousands of screaming beasts, all of them straining at the veil, slashing at it, trying to break free. All the nightmares that would be unleashed into the world if he did not destroy the sword.

Below him Elisha was still falling, plummeting violently into the dark depths, her dress cascading behind her like a curtain of magic. Even as she fell, she righted herself, facing him. *Dante.* Her voice touched his mind, a beautiful, magical voice that filled him with peace for the first time in his life. She held her hand up toward him. *You must take my hand. Only I can show you where the base of the inferno is. It is time to destroy it. It is time for me to die.*

There was such acceptance in her voice, but at the same time, Dante heard something else. Fear. Sadness. Pain. And he knew, with sudden certainty, that his brave, courageous Elisha was a liar.

She didn't want to die either.

Elisha was horrified by the sight of Dante as he hurtled toward her past the creatures scrambling for freedom. Black, tainted blood was oozing from Dante's chest, leaking past the blade that was still buried in his ribs. His skin was ashen. His muscles were locked up, frozen with rigidity.

Elisha. His deep voice filled her mind, and she dragged her gaze off the horror of his injuries. His face was twisted in pain, and yet his eyes were dark and his jaw flexed with determination so fierce it seemed as if he could stop the world from spinning with nothing more than a flick of his finger. The sheer strength of his will seemed to crush the insurmountable odds they were facing, and her throat tightened with emotion as she met his gaze. *You will not die today, Elisha.*

For a split second, she wanted to believe him. She wanted to believe him more than anything she'd ever wanted in her life. But how could she lie to herself and to him? She had to be stronger than that. She wasn't a girl who lived in a world of fantasy. She was a woman who had to be stronger than her heritage. This moment was not about how she felt about him, or what she would want in a different life, in a world where she had options. Her throat tightened with emotions she could not bear to feel, not when she had to find a way to let go of him, and their future.

Instead of pouring out her feelings for him, she simply shook her head and stretched out her hand to him. *Do you see the creatures we're going past? They cannot go free. You know this. We must destroy the sword.* She grabbed his hand as he neared her, and she was shocked by how cold his flesh was. Like ice. Like a man moments from death. Despite her best efforts to be strong, terror plunged through her, and she gripped his hand more tightly. *Damn you, Dante! How could you stab yourself? You have to live!*

His hand convulsed around hers as he pulled them together, somehow summoning strength she couldn't imagine even as they continued to fall, the wind whipping past them. He pulled her close enough to kiss, his mouth fierce and yet gentle at the same time. Tears filled her eyes, tears of longing for what might have been.

Here's the thing, sweetheart, Dante said, pulling back enough to look at her, but not releasing her. He smiled, a smile so tender that she started to cry for real. *You're pretty damn sexy, and I'm not really done with you. It's not going to be* convenient for you to die now, and if I die, then how am I going to have more uncontrollable sex with you?

She stared at him in disbelief, fighting back her tears. *You're thinking of sex right now? Really?*

No. I'm trying to be funny. Lighten the mood. But I'll be honest, making love with you was one of the better moments of my life, so yeah, any moment is a good moment for thinking about it.

She was torn between laughter and tears. *But we're both about to die. The mood is what it is. Not a lot of lightness.*

He pulled her closer against him, his body a buffer against all the chaos around them. *Do you love me?*

Her heart softened, and she knew there was no point in hiding the truth from either of them. *Of course I do.*

He nodded grimly, as if she'd confirmed what he already knew. *So, then, tell me why you die when the sword is destroyed?*

As he asked the question, before she could answer, she felt the wind shift, and knew the moment had come. "Now!" she shouted. "We have to stop our descent now!"

Without hesitation, responding instantly to her command, Dante called out his spear with a crack and a flash of black light. He slammed it into the nearest wall. It plunged deep and jerked them both to a stop, the steel blade bowing under the weight of their bodies. But Dante held onto it with surreal strength, his free arm still wrapped around her. She realized suddenly that the sword of darkness was no longer fused to his hand. It had released him once the veil had been severed. Or maybe the fact it was still lodged in his chest was enough of a connection between them.

Moving with agility beyond comprehension, given the depths of his injuries and the blade still in his body, he swung them to the side, into a crevice in the wall. She fell to her knees beside him, and put her hand on the sword. "Please, can't we take this out—"

"No." He put his hand on hers. "I have a bad feeling

about what will happen if we pull it free."

Below them, the darkness seemed to ferment and boil, and streaks of purple light began to shoot past them. "My mother," whispered Elisha in horror. "She's coming. We must go!"

She scrambled to her feet, slip-sliding over the rocks, Dante behind her. "The source of the inferno is over here," she shouted, scrambling along the rough surface. "You just have to plunge the sword into it."

"Why do you die when the sword is destroyed?" Dante yelled again.

She found the opening in the rocky cliff that she'd been searching for, and ducked into it, Dante right behind her. "Because I'm linked to the sword now," she said, even as the sense of loss overwhelmed her. Now that she had found hope, love and kindness in Dante, she wasn't ready to die. He was a gift, the light in a life that had been so dark, that suddenly made life worth fighting for. But it was too late. There was no other choice.

Then she saw it. A silent, black pool that looked like ink. From it billowed vapors so translucent they were almost invisible, the vapors that would twist and contort when they got to the earth's surface. It was the inferno's source, the thing that would destroy the sword and free the world from this threat. It was also the thing that would kill her, and tear her away from the man she loved, and the son she would never know. "I linked myself to the sword to get out of the queen's darkness, so if it is destroyed, it takes me with it. I can't support myself out in the earth realm—"

Dante grabbed her suddenly and flung her back against the wall. His face was twisted in pain, and he was breathing heavily. With a roar of fury, he grabbed the hilt of the sword and pulled it out of his chest. His scream of agony filled the tunnel, and she cried out as he fell to his knees.

She went down beside him, holding his head off the

rocks. "Dante," she whispered, tears streaming down her cheeks. "How can this be our fate?"

He was on his side now, his chest heaving desperately for air. "The curse. The darkness. Does it hurt you? Would my father's curse hurt you?"

She frowned, trying to grasp his question when all she wanted to do was cry and mourn the loss that was so imminent. "No, of course not, it's who I am—"

He gripped her wrist. "The earth...it supports me. I can live in the earth realm." He could barely get the words out. "I can provide the life support that sword was giving you."

Purple flashes began to fill the tunnel, and she sensed her mother was rising to the veil. "Dante, we have to go." Unable to stop the tears, she grabbed him under the arms and began to drag him across the uneven ground toward the pool. "Rohan won't be able to hold it closed against her."

Dante's head lolled back, his body weak, so weak. The curse was up to his chest now, blackened and twisting, mixing with the blow from the sword. She couldn't believe he was still alive, that he was still hanging on. "You can do it," she whispered, as they reached the pool. "You can live. I know you can. You must, for our son."

"No." He was inert on the ground, barely moving, but his eyes were fixed on hers. "I won't live, and you won't either. Not alone. Only together." His eyes fluttered shut. "The runes," he whispered. "The runes keep us apart. We are bonded by blood. My energy runs in you. Yours runs in me. If we combine... you give me your protection against the queen's darkness and I give you my ability to live in the earth realm. We help each other."

She stared at him, as sudden, fragile hope flared inside her. "Or," she said, "we give each other our vulnerabilities, and we end up with no protections from anything."

His eyes opened a slit. "Then we die."

"And our son?"

"If we don't try it, we die anyway. For him, we must try. For us, we must try." His voice faded, too rough and weak. *I love you, Elisha. That gives me strength. Help me.*

There were screams from outside the tunnel, and suddenly orange flames and blue light reflected on the walls. "They've reached Rohan and Zach," he said. "Now!"

She looked into the eyes of the man who had given her hope. The warrior so strong that the sword had chosen him. She thought of the life she'd lived in hell, and the son she didn't want to ever give up. *I love you, no matter what.*

And I love you. Then, not taking his gaze off her, he grabbed the sword. He was weak, too weak to lift it, and she helped him. Together, they dragged it down his arms, tearing off the flesh that carried the runes that prevented the *sheva* bond from developing. She cried for his pain, but he didn't even flinch. He was simply focused on her, his eyes blazing with so much emotion that her heart seemed to come alive. The moment the last rune was cut away, something seemed to surge to life within her. Suddenly, she felt like she was a part of Dante. She could feel his pain, his courage, his guilt, and so much love that it blinded her.

Now! Together, they grabbed the sword and hoisted it over the edge of the pool. For a split second, it hovered over the glassy surface, fighting their efforts, and she thought they weren't going to be able to penetrate the surface.

"In the name of love!" Dante bellowed as he leapt to his feet, throwing all his weight onto the sword. With a crack that shook the very earth, it plunged into the pool, shattering the surface of the water. The walls shook, and the earth screamed. Noxious fumes flooded the small cave and streamed out the entrance. Screams of anguish and fury filled the air, and the mountain shook violently, rocks tumbling down around them.

Triumph rushed through her and she grabbed his arm. "Can you feel that? You did it! The veil is closing!"

Dante gasped and fell to the earth, his flesh blackened

and twisted as the curse took him. "Dante!" She grabbed for him, but at the same moment, sudden, debilitating pain overwhelmed her, and she cried out in agony as she fell beside him.

Pain filled her, a searing of her very soul, and she knew the bonding between her and Dante hadn't succeeded. She was still dying. They were both still dying. *It hadn't worked.*

CHAPTER TWELVE

Elisha shielded her head against the onslaught of rocks, her body twisting in agony as life was ripped from it. *Elisha!* Dante's arm wrapped around her, and he dragged her beneath him.

His face was twisted in pain as he tucked her underneath his body, shielding her from the cascading rocks with his own flesh. Even in death, he was trying to protect her. *It didn't work, Dante—*

We're not done yet. His voice filled her mind again, the same words that he'd spoken before, only this time they spread through her like a golden healing light. His voice was full of wonder and love, and he filled her with his heart and his spirit. *Mine to you. Yours to me. Bonded by blood, by spirit and by soul, we are one. No distance too far, no enemy too powerful, no sacrifice too great. I'll always find you. I'll always protect you. No matter what the cost. I am yours as you are mine.*

And just as before, the words came to her as well, but this time their importance filled her, and she felt the weight and power of each word as she spoke it. *Mine to you. Yours to me. Bonded by blood, by spirit and by soul, we are one. No distance too far, no enemy too powerful, no sacrifice too great. I'll always find you. I'll always keep you safe. No matter what the cost. I am yours as you are mine.*

My dearest Elisha. Dante's body shuddered above her, and he sank more heavily onto her. *Merge with me. Let us share our strengths and our healing.*

She felt his soul open to hers, and she began to cry as he enveloped her with his strength and protection, a safety net so powerful that she knew she was protected. For the first time in her life, she was safe. Her body was still screaming in agony, and her cells were still dying, but she opened her spirit to him, welcoming him, wrapping herself around his soul and letting him fill her with his healing strength. And as she did so, she sensed the dark power of the curse eating away at him, a dark magic that she was born of. Instinctively, she reached for it, welcomed it, and soothed it. It recognized her and released him, sliding into her body, into the home where it was safe, where it belonged, freeing Dante.

Relief rushed through her, and she closed her eyes, sagging against the rocky ground. Dante would survive. Their son would survive.

Dante shuddered once again, and then his weight grew even heavier as he collapsed on top of her. *And now it is your turn. Take what I give you, my love.* As he spoke, she felt a warm, healing strength pulsing through her, much like what she'd felt when Dante and the others had brought her back after Rohan had killed her. Only this time, it was richer and stronger. A beautiful, powerful energy that flooded her body with strength, healing, and life force. He was giving her his humanity, his energy, and his very life, anchoring her. As he did it, the pain in her body began to recede, her heart began to beat again, and her lungs filled with air.

It worked?

Elisha. Dante sagged against her, wrapping his arms around her as he held her.

She clung tightly to him, terrified to let go, terrified to lose their connection. But even as she held onto him, her arms were trembling. She was still so weak, too weak. *Dante? What's going on?*

I'm still bleeding from the blow to the heart. I need to heal that. I need to go into a healing sleep. I can't hold us both alive until I do that. Come with me. Now.

Sleep? Now? Here? Terror began to beat at her as she opened her eyes, looking past his shoulder. There were rocks all around them, trapping them. Which side of the veil were they on? Were they in the queen's darkness, or had it retreated? *I don't—*

Then suddenly, a tiny orange fireball squeezed between the rocks. It hovered above them, twinkling brightly. Disbelief flooded her. "Dante? Is that Zach?"

Dante groaned and lifted his head. "That damn kid better not kill us." Then he tucked her more tightly beneath him and they both shielded their heads.

The explosion was as violent and overdone as any of the others Zach had caused, sending the earth outward as it exploded. For a split second, emptiness and space hovered around them, and then the mountain began to fall for real—

Suddenly strong hands yanked Dante off her, and she opened her eyes to see Rohan holding her. Zach had thrown Dante over his shoulder. No words were exchanged, and their two rescuers raced down the tunnel that Zach's explosion had opened. They had only a split second before the cavern collapsed and crushed them all.

As they ran, weakness began to flood her again, and she knew she needed Dante. He had connected them through their blood bond and brought her back from the edge, but it hadn't been enough. She needed him to sustain her. She looked over, and saw his face was pale and pinched. The wound on his chest was raw and gaping, oozing too much blood. He was dying faster than he could heal himself, and so was she. "Rohan," she gasped. "Dante's dying!"

He didn't even look at her. He just kept running, faster than she thought was possible for a man to move. "I know."

Then they reached the opening to the tunnel and the warriors began to climb. Elisha fought to stay conscious, but each step they took seemed to drain the last of the energy from her. It was too late. It wasn't enough. She was still going to die, and so was he. "Dante," she gasped, reaching out blindly to him, not even knowing where he was.

I'm here. His hand found hers, gripping tightly, and she felt his warmth flood her again. Not enough to save her, but she knew she would die with a smile in her heart, because Dante would always be a part of her soul...but he had to live for their son. "Fight for him," she whispered. "Fight for him, Dante. *You must live.*"

Dante fought to stay conscious as Zach and Rohan carried them out, but his need for a healing sleep was so strong he knew he would succumb within moments. He wouldn't go into it without Elisha. He had to take her with him. *Stay with me, Elisha. Stay with me!*

There was no answer, but he could feel the warmth of her spirit, reassuring him that she was still with him, still hanging on. He focused entirely on her, sending her the last remnants of his energy, the bare fragments of life he still contained.

"Stop wasting your energy on her," Rohan shouted at him as the warriors scaled the walls of the now-silent pit, climbing rapidly to the surface of the earth. "Heal yourself! You're going to die!"

"I need Elisha," Dante gasped. "Need to save her."

"You need to save yourself!"

Then suddenly, they were free, back on the surface, fresh air filling their lungs. The night was cool and clear, all vestiges of the roaring fire gone, leaving behind nothing but charred earth and smoking vegetation. "Put me down," Dante gasped. "Bring her to me."

Zach set him down, but Rohan stood before him, still

holding Elisha. Her head was lolled back against his shoulder, her body limp and frail. "Look at her arms," Rohan said. "Look at them!"

Dante's pulse thundered when he saw his spears etched on her arms. The brands weren't complete, indicating that they hadn't done all the bonding stages. He had no idea what stages they'd done, or how many of the five they'd completed. All he knew was that it hadn't been enough to complete the bond and trigger the fate that would destroy them, but they were connected enough that he could take her into his healing sleep and save her. An intense sense of rightness coursed through him for the marks on her arms. "She is mine. Bring her to me."

"Don't you get it?" Rohan didn't move. "She must die. You must let her go. She's the queen's successor. Her son will carry more power than both of you combined. It must end now. The circle must be broken."

"No!" Dante surged to his feet, staggering as weakness assaulted him. His foot was whole again, but his chest was too damaged. He could feel his heart laboring with each beat, fading fast. "She is mine—"

"She's your *sheva!*" Rohan snapped. "She will destroy you! She must die!'

"She saved me!"

"Her legacy is to save you! You cannot let her destroy the earth." Rohan called out his sword in a wild explosion of white light. "She must die—"

"No!" There was an outraged howl, and a fireball slammed into Rohan, knocking him backward. He dropped Elisha as he fell, and Dante caught her, collapsing to his knees as his body drained the last of his energy.

Zach leapt over them and inserted himself between them and Rohan. Fire spewed off him as he continued to hammer fireballs at Rohan so relentlessly the other warrior could not recover enough to fight back. "No more innocents die," he shouted. "No more women. You heal her. I will hold

Rohan off. Go!"

Dante didn't hesitate. He could feel the younger warrior's passion and anger, and he knew it was strong enough to sustain him. Rohan was solid and stoic, but no match for the nightmares haunting Zach. Without another word, Dante pulled Elisha against him and closed his eyes, falling instantly into the healing sleep, trusting the wild, untrained, undisciplined warrior to keep him safe from the man who was his best friend.

Peace.

It was the first thought that came to her mind. Peace. Her mind. Her body. Her soul. They were all at peace. Was this death? It didn't feel like death. It felt like she was cocooned in a protected place of safety and warmth. She could feel life pulsing through her, a warmth that was unfamiliar, but beautiful.

Elisha?

Dante's familiar voice caressed her. Confusion echoed through her, but then she became aware that it was his body creating the cocoon. His arms were around her, his legs tangled with hers. His breath was warm on her cheek. It was his heat and strength encircling her, infusing her body with a sense of safety and warmth that she'd never felt before.

Hope fought to surface, and slowly, afraid to be wrong, she opened her eyes.

Dante was smiling down at her, his dark eyes still swirling with the shadows he always carried. But there was a softness to them as well, a humanity that was just for her. She smiled back and touched his whiskered jaw. He was real, not her imagination. "Did we do it?" she whispered.

He smiled. "We did. For now."

Disbelief filled her, and tears suddenly clogged her throat. Together, they held each other, the silent embrace representing all the words she couldn't articulate. "We have each other? Really?"

He pulled away slightly, brushing her hair back. "We have each other. We really do."

She nodded, pressing her lips together to fight off the tears. It was too much, the emotions she was feeling. Love. Relief. Hope. *I love you.*

Not half as much as I love you. He kissed her then, the most beautiful, tender kiss full of love and promises that filled her soul so completely that suddenly, finally, all the pain and fear accumulated in her life seemed to vanish, chased aside by their mutual love.

Dante broke the kiss and smiled down at her then, his eyes twinkling with the same happiness and love filling her so completely. "We must be careful, though."

"Why?" She tangled her fingers in his hair. She could spend days in his arms, exploring his body and his soul. Now that the world wasn't crashing down around them, she wanted to stop running and start living. She wanted to breathe deeply. She wanted to be with this man who had become her world. She wanted to learn every secret he had and find out all there was to know about him.

"Because, as it turns out, you really are my *sheva.*" He pressed his lips to her forearm, and she saw the partial outline of his brand on her arm. The silver lines were beautiful, a symbol of their connection. "If we complete the bond, we will trigger the fate that destroys our kind."

"I'm your *sheva.*" The words sounded perfect. She traced her fingers over the brands, marveling at how right and beautiful it felt to carry Dante's marks. After all they had been through, she could not muster any fear about linking herself to him. It was the way it should be, and exactly where she wanted to be. "Can't we just decide we won't do the final stages?"

He shook his head. "No one has ever been strong enough to bond partially and stop it. It's too strong."

"Like the sword was too strong?" She remembered all

too well his refusal to accept the impossible.

He grinned. "It's stronger than the sword, my love."

"Not stronger than us." She put her hand over the brand on his arm.

"Nothing is ever impossible," he agreed, but his eyes were weighted with the reality of what they were facing.

She met his gaze, accepting the challenge ahead of them, but refusing to be overwhelmed by it. "So, what do we do?"

"We live in the present, and we take it one day at a time." He pressed a kiss to her lips. *But right now, we have each other, for however long we can hold onto it.*

She nodded. After all she had been through, after what she had been prepared to face, every moment she had with Dante was a gift. "One day at time," she echoed. She could live one day at a time, so why look beyond that? Each day with him was all she could want.

He grinned, a smile that seemed to light up his face and strip a century of hard living from his features. "I love you, my princess."

"And I love you—"

"She will destroy the earth," Rohan said darkly. "As will your son."

Elisha twisted in Dante's arms as he sat up, helping her rise with him. Rohan was sitting on a charred tree trunk, his cloak still draped over his head. For a split second, she had an image of a shadowed face, of haunted eyes, and she wondered if she'd caught a glimpse of him when he'd carried her out.

Zach was pacing in front of Rohan, covered only in a charred piece of clothing draped around his waist, a concession to modesty that she suspected was for her benefit. "You're wrong, you know," Zach said. "She's not evil. You are, Rohan."

Dante held up his hand to silence the discussion. "She lives. For now." His gaze met Rohan's. "Your visions do not always come true. You know this."

"This one is powerful. Terrible things will come from

this woman. Terrible things will come from your son. And yet you have bound yourself to her." Rohan was still sitting on the upended tree, no longer trying to kill her, as if he'd accepted that today was not the day for him to get to her, not with Dante and Zach as her guardians.

Dante's gaze glittered. "You would have me choose death, instead? She holds my curse at bay. We need each other to live."

Rohan was silent for a long moment, then he stood up and strode across the charred earth, staring out across the valley.

Zach studied Dante. "I heard the Calydon speak," he said. "The one who killed my family."

Dante pulled Elisha more tightly against him and studied the youth. "What did you hear?"

"He said you were the new leader of the Order." Zach went down on one knee and bowed his head. "I offer my services to you. There can be no more rogues destroying innocents. No more suffering. No more pain."

"I turned him down, as you know."

Zach raised his head. "Then give me the mantle. I have proven myself today. I will kill friends. I will kill enemies. I will strike down any rogue who does what Louis did to my family. I will do it."

A cold chill went over Dante as he looked into Zach's eyes and saw the rawness of his emotions and the depth of his commitment. He knew he was looking into the face of a man who would never forget what had happened to those he had loved. A warrior who would never fall to the allure of power at the cost of what was right. Zach was a Calydon who was safe from the contamination that had destroyed his father, because Zach's grief and anguish would never, ever let him forget. "You can't control your fire," Dante pointed out. "You're a liability to everyone around you."

Zach narrowed his eyes. "I will never make that kind of

mistake. I will never let my fire harm an innocent. *Never.*"

And Dante believed him. For the first time in his life, Dante had met a warrior worthy of being in the Order. "Very well."

Zach's eyes widened. "Very well, what? I'm the new leader of the Order?"

"No!" Rohan strode back over to them, his body rigid. "He is too young," he snapped. "He needs a leader to guide him." Rohan pointed at Dante, his muscular arm taut, the brand on his arm almost vibrating with the intensity of his words. "It has to be you, Dante. It must be you."

"Me?" For a split second, Dante had a vision of taking up the mantle, of making the Order what it should have been. Excitement pulsed through him, and then he thought of his father, and what he'd become. "No." Dante looked at Elisha. "I chose to bond myself with a woman," he said quietly. "I'm the one who will go rogue. I'm the one who will need to be killed. I'm the one who's not worthy—"

"Really? Are you so certain?" This time, it was Elisha who challenged him, her shoulders pulled back with the same courageous strength he admired so much. "You found a way to save me, yourself, and all the innocents. You see solutions where there are none." She laid her hand on his chest, over his heart. "You killed your father to save others. You controlled the sword that no one could manage. You used your love for me to your advantage. How can you doubt your strength? Your courage?" She gestured to the charred earth around them, signs of a battle they had barely won. "It doesn't end today, Dante. It will continue. Someone has to stop it. Someone has to rebuild what was lost." She met his gaze. "And that someone is you."

Dante looked around at the three people watching him so intently. He thought of the evil that had filled that inferno. Of the innocents like his mother who had died at the hands of his father. He thought of Zach's grief at the loss of his family.

"The Order will survive," Rohan said. "Power fills a void. If it is not you who leads, it will be someone else. Someone not strong or wise enough to know what needs to be done."

Dante studied Zach, and he saw the truth Rohan spoke. Zach would make sure the Order continued. Zach, who was so volatile and angry, was roiling with power so raw that it could easily destroy him if he wasn't trained. But at the same time, Dante now understood where his father had failed. Unlike his father, he understood what it took to make a Calydon worthy of being Order. He needed warriors whose emotions were ragged and raw, so intense the warriors could barely survive them. He needed Calydons whose emotions and baggage were so horrific that they would never, ever forget what mattered.

Dante was not worthy of leading the Order, but he could see now that it could be possible to find warriors who could live the creed that the Order was founded upon. He could rebuild, and then take himself out before he, too, fell to the dangers of what he was. He looked at Rohan, the friend he'd had for so long, who had survived so much with him. "When it's time, you will wield the sword that kills me."

Rohan nodded. "It will be my honor."

Elisha let out a soft sound of protest, and he looked over at her. *For as long as we have, my love.*

Tears filled her eyes, and she took his hand, holding it to her chest. *For as long as we have.* She smiled then, a tremulous expression of courage. "But just so you know, I'm going to fight for that to be forever."

He grinned, a new sense of hope and resolution filling him. With Elisha by his side, who knew what he could become? "Forever sounds damn good to me."

He knew they would fight to the end, for themselves, for their son, for a world where innocents did not have to die. Still holding her hand, he looked at the two warriors before him, and his smile faded. "It looks like we're going to have an induction ceremony," he said. "Zach, you in?"

The younger warrior nodded, his face becoming grim and determined. "Always."

Dante nodded, and then to his surprise, Rohan knelt beside Zach, bowing his head the same way. Dante went still, staring at his friend. "You want to be Order?"

Rohan raised his head. "There is no warrior besides you that I would follow. I swear my allegiance to you, until the day I must strike you down."

For a split second, Dante hesitated. Rohan was powerful and ruthless, a warrior who was always willing to sacrifice innocents for the greater good. He was a man his father would have chosen. Was he also a man that Dante could trust?

Rohan raised his head, and Dante knew that Rohan sensed his hesitation.

"What do you see for yourself?" Dante asked. "What do you see for your future?"

"I cannot see my own."

For a moment, there was silence. Then Elisha's soft voice echoed in his mind as she squeezed his hand. *He has great pain,* she said softly. *Tremendous pain. Pain beyond words and comprehension. I felt it when he was carrying me.*

He looked over at Elisha, at the woman he loved, at the woman that Rohan believed should die. There was more to Rohan than he knew, even after all the years he'd spent trapped in hell with him. Was it enough? Did Rohan carry enough suffering to drive him down the right path, or would his discipline lead him down the road to corruption and dishonor?

Then he thought of that night. That one horrific night in the pit. The incident he hadn't even told Elisha about. He remembered what Rohan had done. And he knew that he had to give him the chance. Rohan could be the key to it all...or their downfall.

Dante knew how dark the world was. He knew that his own son and the woman he loved were linked to an evil beyond anything they had ever seen before. If Rohan could deliver, they would need him. He looked at Rohan. *If you fail, I promise to be the one to strike you down, my friend.*

Rohan nodded once, an understanding of who they each were, and the power that lay within them both. *Agreed.*

Then so it shall be. Still holding Elisha's hand, he called out his spear, standing above the two warriors who were the only hope for the future, for innocence, for life. He didn't know whether it was the right choice, whether he would fail, whether they would fail, but as he now understood, he had to try. "We shall begin."

SNEAK PEEK: DARKNESS UNLEASHED

THE ORDER OF THE BLADE
Available Now

Ryland spun around, engaging all his preternatural senses as he searched the graveyard for Catherine. He knew she had to be close. He'd touched her backpack just before she'd vanished right in front of him.

"Catherine!" he shouted again. He'd been so close. Where the hell was she? All he could sense were the deaths of all the people in the graveyard. Women, children, old men, young men, good people, scum who had taken their demented values to the grave with them. The spirits were thick and heavy in the graveyard, souls that had not moved on to their place of rest.

They circled him, trying to penetrate his barriers, seeking asylum in the creature that would be their doom. "No," he said to them. "I'm not your savior." Not by a long shot. He was about as far from their savior as it was possible to be.

Dismissing them, Ryland focused more directly on Catherine, opening his senses to the night, but as much as he tried to concentrate, he couldn't keep the vision of her out of his head. He'd finally seen her up close. She'd been mere inches away, the angel who had filled his thoughts for so long. Her hair was gold. Gold. It must have been tucked up under a hat when he'd seen her before, but now? It was unlike anything he'd ever seen before. He'd been riveted by the sight of it streaming behind her as she ran, the golden highlights glistening in the dark as if she'd been lit from within.

Her gait had been smooth and agile, but he'd sensed the sheer effort she'd had to expend during the run. Another few feet, and he would have caught up to her easily, but she'd sensed him while he'd still been a quarter mile away, giving her a head start that had gotten her to the graveyard first.

Shit. He had to focus and find her. Summoning his rigid control to focus on his task, Ryland crouched down and placed his hand on the dirt path where he'd last seen her. The ground was humming with the energy of death, but again, he couldn't untangle her trail from all the others. He realized that she'd mingled her own scent of death with those of all the other spirits, making it impossible for him to track her. He grinned as he rested his forearm on his quad and surveyed the small cemetery. "I'm impressed," he said aloud. "You're good."

There was no response, but he had the distinct sensation that she was watching him.

Slowly, he rose to his feet. "My name is Ryland Samuels," he said. "I'm a member of the Order of the Blade, the group of warriors that you protect. I'm here to offer you my protection and bring you into our safekeeping."

Again, there was no answer, but suddenly threaded through the tendrils of death was the cold filament of fear. Not just a superficial apprehension, but the kind of deep, penetrating fear that would bring a person to their knees and render them powerless. Fear of him? Or of the fact he said he wanted to take her with him? Swearing, Ryland turned in a slow circle, searching for where she might be. "There's no need to be afraid of me. I would never hurt an angel."

The fear thickened, like the thorns of a dying rose pricking his skin.

Ryland moved slowly toward the far corner, and smiled when he felt the terror grow stronger. She might be able to hide death, but there was no cover for the terror that was hers alone. He was clearly getting closer to her. "Look into my eyes," he said softly. "I don't hurt angels."

There was a whisper of a sound behind him, and he felt the cold drift of fingers across his back. She was touching him.

He froze, not daring to turn around, even though his heartbeat had suddenly accelerated a thousand-fold. Her touch was so faint, almost as if it were her spirit that was examining him, not her own flesh. Was she merely invisible right now, or had she abandoned her physical existence completely and traveled to some spiritual plane? He had no idea what she was capable of. All he knew was that he felt like he never wanted to move away from this spot, not as long as she was touching him. He wanted to stay right where he was and never break the connection.

He closed his eyes, breathing in the sensation of her touch as her fingers traced down his arm, over his jacket. What was she looking for? Was she reading his aura? Searching for the truth of his claim that he would not hurt her? She would get nowhere trying to get a read on him. He never allowed anyone to see who he truly was, not even an angel of death.

But even as he thought it, he made no move to resist, his pulse quickening in anticipation as her touch trailed toward his bare hand. Would she brush her fingers over his skin? Would he feel the touch of an angel for the first time in a thousand years? He felt his soul begin to strain, reaching for this gift only she could give him.

He tracked every inch of movement as her hand moved lower toward his bare skin. Past his elbow. To the cuff of his sleeve. Then he felt it. Her fingers on the back of his hand. His flesh seemed to ignite under her touch. A wave of angelic serenity and beauty cascaded through his soul, like a breath of great relief easing a thousand years of tension from his lungs.

At the same time, there was a dangerous undercurrent beneath the beauty, a darkness that he recognized as death. A thousand souls seemed to dance through his mind, spirits lodged in the depths of her existence. Her emotions flooded him. Fear. Regret. Determination. Love. A sense of being trapped.

Trapped? He understood that one well. Far too well.

Instinctively, he flipped his hand over, wrapping his fingers around hers, not to trap her, but to offer her his protection from a hell that still drove every choice he made.

He heard her suck in her breath, and she went still, not pulling away from him. Her hand was cold. Her fingers were small and delicate, like fragile blossoms that would snap under a stiff breeze. A hand that needed support and help.

Ryland snapped his eyes open but there was no one standing in front of him. He looked down and could see only his own hand, folded around air. He couldn't see her, but she was there, her hand in his, not pulling away. "Show yourself to me," he said. "I won't hurt you."

Her hand jerked back, and a sense of loss assailed him as he lost his grip on her. "No!" He reached for her, but his hands just drifted through air. "Catherine," he urged, as he strained to get a sense of her. "I—"

SNEAK PEEK: DARKNESS ARISEN

THE ORDER OF THE BLADE
Available Now

Alice's heart began to race as she saw Ian dive through the waves in pursuit of her, his powerful body breaking through the white caps with minimal effort. Just like before, the mere anticipation of his nearness sent waves of awareness and desire rushing through her...along with a pulsing sense of danger.

He was too determined, and the look on his teammate's face too arrogant as he followed Ian through the waves. She didn't know what they wanted from her, but she knew she couldn't afford it.

She quickly turned her back on them and moved to the edge of the rock, scanning the surface of the ocean for the bumps that were too sleek and too misty to be natural. The pearl was still cold in her hand, clenched there despite all that had happened since she'd thrown herself into the water.

The Mageaan had known she was in the ocean. They'd tried to kill her, which meant they were nearby, or they had been at least. Were they still around? Trying to ignore the sound of Ian getting closer to her, Alice inched toward the edge of the rock. She opened her hand and looked at the pearl. Glittering streaks of red, orange, crimson and silver sliced across its surface, like the clouds at sunset on the eve of a hurricane. "Please let this work," she whispered. It was such a risk to reveal that she had the pearl. To give it away was to surrender the one safeguard she had against an eternity of hell, against the future that Ian seemed to be pushing her towards.

But without the help of the creatures in the water below,

she had no chance to find Catherine. The Mageaan owned the oceans. They knew everything and everyone that passed through their waters. They would know where Catherine was, but they would never reveal it. Not to an outsider. Not to someone who represented all they had lost...unless she had something to offer them that was more than they could resist.

The pearl was that item. She might be able to convince the Mageaan to trade information for the jewel. Of course, once she reached Catherine... A cold chill rippled through her. How would she manage that without Flynn? She couldn't do that on her own.

No. She couldn't worry about that now. None of it mattered if she couldn't find Catherine in the first place, and the Mageaan were the only ones who would know how to find the lair that was hidden, obscured by magic and tricks so that no one could find it. No one but the man who had created it... and those who haunted the ocean.

She carefully held the pearl up between her thumb and index finger so that the moon's blue-green rays seemed to refract through it, bringing it to life. She glanced over her shoulder and saw Ian was almost to the rock, his muscled shoulders churning powerfully through the whitecaps as he neared.

Crap! He was almost to the rock! Alice quickly extended her hand out over the ocean. It was risky, exposing it like that, but she was over a hundred feet above the water. The Mageaan were ocean bound, and they would not be able to steal it from her up here. "I have one of the Pearls of Lycath," she shouted. "I will trade it for your help!" The wind seemed to strip the words from her mouth and thrust them out across the water, reverberating again and again. "You can have it," she yelled, even as fear rippled through her at the idea of giving it up. "I will offer it freely!"

A haunted call sounded across the ocean, making the hairs on her arms stand up. Alice searched the water, and she saw a faint drift of mist forming on the horizon. Excitement shot through her. Was that the Mageaan? "I have the pearl," she yelled again, holding it out for them to see. "It's genuine. I will trade it for your help!"

The mist swirled closer and thicker, and the water churned more violently as the wind began to howl. Her hair slashed her cheeks, her clothes snapped in the gusts. On the edges of the wind, Alice thought she heard the sound of a woman screaming. Dozens of women screaming, the kind of screams that heralded a brutal death coming for them. Their torment was horrific, the pain of souls being ripped apart for an eternity of suffering.

She froze, horrified by the sound. Oh, God. What was that? Was that the Mageaan? If it was, it was so much worse than she'd expected. She'd heard the stories. She'd been warned a thousand times. But there had been no way to comprehend the depths of such suffering. The edge to their screams was like a blade shredding the night. Was that her future? Was that what she would become without the pearl to protect her?

Real terror rippled through her. I can't do this. Her hand faltered, and she started to lower it—

A violent gust of wind slammed into her shoulders from behind, thrusting her forward off the edge of the rock. She screamed as she was thrust into the air, and then the wind tore the pearl from her grasp. "No!"

Anguish tore through her as she lunged for it, but her hand closed on empty air as the pearl plummeted down toward the water, the wind howling in triumph, as if the Mageaan themselves had compelled it to help them. Beneath her swelled the mist, but it was no longer white. It was a seething, frothing purple and black pool of poison—

"Hey!" A hand clamped around her wrist, jerking her backwards.

Alice gasped as she ricocheted back against the side of the rock, her body slamming into hard granite, suspended above the tumultuous ocean by one arm. She looked up, and her heart stuttered when she saw Ian down on one knee on the top of the rock, his fingers locked around her wrist. "No, no!" She tugged at her arm. "Let me go! I have to get the pearl! I dropped it in the water!" Frantic, she kicked at the rock, trying to tear herself out of his grasp.

"Hey!" He tightened his grip, ocean water streaming down his arm over his hand. "A pearl? You're serious? You'll never find a pearl down there. That ocean is trying to kill you."

"I don't care! Let me go!" Without the pearl, she had nothing: no future for herself and no way to find Catherine. "I have to get it!" Frantic, she twisted around to search the frothing depths, but her heart sank when she saw the ocean churning beneath her. Hate-filled green and purple swells fighting to get to her, to reclaim the victim they'd lost once, and deadly mist swirled over the surface of the water.

She couldn't survive that. There was no way she could reclaim her pearl from that. Despair coursed through her, utter despair. It was gone. Without it, Catherine was lost to her. One moment of fear and hesitation for her own stupid life, and she'd lost her chance. Frustration and guilt burned through Alice, and all the fight drained from her body. She hung limply from Ian's grasp, the cold wet rock pressing against her as she dangled over her death. This couldn't happen again. She couldn't fail again.

"Alice." Ian's voice was low. Impatient. "Look at me."

She pulled her gaze off the ocean and looked up, compelled by the urgency in his voice. The moment she met his intense gaze, awareness coursed through her. Awareness of the man, of herself, of something more personal than it should have been. Fear rippled through her, fear of the warrior who held her wrist.

"I've never met someone more likely to die than I am," he said conversationally, as if he wasn't the only thing standing between her and a nightmare. "It's damned inconvenient."

She met his gaze, her jaw jutting out. "I'm not afraid of death."

"No, I can see that." One eyebrow was raised, but his eyes were cool and calculating. Water was streaming down his arm over hers, but his grip was tight and secure. "What is it that you are afraid of, Alice Shaw?"

What was she afraid of? Unbidden, the memory flashed into her mind. Her mother, blood pouring from a wound in her chest, laboring to breathe. Her mother's blond hair matted with blood and dirt, her bright blue eyes glazed over with the onset of death, her lips parted as she fought to share those last words while Alice sat there, inches away, unable to do the one simple thing that would have saved her life—

Ian's gaze sharpened. *Who is that in your mind, sheva? Who died like that?* His voice was soft and gentle, reaching deep into her soul, tearing away at the protective shields that enabled her to get through her life every day.

She quickly stiffened, and shook her head. "Leave me alone."

Ian's eyes narrowed. "Maybe you should save that request for after I pull you back up."

Alice grimaced, and glanced down, the sea was still churning beneath her. Waves splashed up, reaching for her ankles. Instinctively, she pulled her feet up, bracing them against the rock. "You have a point."

"As I thought." Ian grinned then, and braced himself on the rock. "Ready?"

She met his gaze, fighting not to be swallowed up by his piercing stare. "Ready." She dug her toes into the rock.

"On three." He cocked an eyebrow. "One." He held his other hand out to her.

After a split second of hesitation, she reached up and took his hand. His grip was strong around her wrists again. Damn, the man was powerful. How was that fair? He could probably take down the world, and she, the angel of life, couldn't save even a single person, no matter how simple a task it would be to help them.

He nodded. "Two."

She wrapped her fingers around his wrist, and electricity jumped between them. Dammit. Why hadn't things lessened between them? Why was he still affecting her like this?

"Three." He gave a curt nod and pulled.

She pushed off the rock as he shifted his body, easily swinging her to the top of the rock. Her bare feet landed silently on the rock, her toes tiny and pale next to the heavy boots he was still wearing. "Swimming's easier without boots," she said, trying desperately to put distance between them.

He shrugged. "I was in a rush. You were getting away."

There was that sense of being hunted by him again. Alice instinctively pulled out of his grasp. "What do you want from me?"

Ian went still for a moment, and his gaze bore down on her. She felt pressure in her mind as he tried to break past her barriers, connecting with her too intimately. She stiffened immediately and folded her arms over her chest, raising her chin as she faced him, fighting against the swirl of emotion he aroused in her. "You're not stalking me because of the soul mate thing, are you? Because I'm not yours—"

"Yes, you are." His response was instant and unyielding, and she felt her pulse quicken in response.

She couldn't afford to belong to him. She didn't want to crave him so badly that she felt like her own soul would burst into violent flames if he walked away from her...but she did. It was like he'd ignited a raging fire within her, one that he stoked ever higher with each touch, with each word, with each kiss.

And as a smug grin spread over his face, she knew that he was well aware of exactly how he affected her.

"Damn you, Ian," she snapped.

He grinned more broadly, and she suddenly realized that she'd just laid down a challenge that he was delighted to accept.

SNEAK PEEK: ICE

ALASKA HEAT
Available Now

Kaylie's hands were shaking as she rifled through her bag, searching for her yoga pants. She needed the low-slung black ones with a light pink stripe down the side. The cuffs were frayed from too many wearings to the grocery store late at night for comfort food, and they were her go-to clothes when she couldn't cope. Like now.

She couldn't find them.

"Come on!" Kaylie grabbed her other suitcase and dug through it, but they weren't there. "Stupid pants! I can't—" A sob caught at her throat and she pressed her palms to her eyes, trying to stifle the swell of grief. "Sara—"

Her voice was a raw moan of pain, and she sank to the thick shag carpet. She bent over as waves of pain, of loneliness, of utter grief shackled her. For her parents, her brother, her family and now Sara—

Dear God, she was all alone.

"Dammit, Kaylie! Get up!" she chided herself. She wrenched herself to her feet. "I can do this." She grabbed a pair of jeans and a silk blouse off the top of her bag and turned toward the bathroom. One step at a time. A shower would make her feel better.

She walked into the tiny bathroom, barely noticing the heavy wood door as she stepped inside and flicked the light switch. Two bare light bulbs flared over her head, showing a rustic bathroom with an ancient footed tub and a raw wood vanity with a battered porcelain sink. A tiny round window was on her right. It was small enough to keep out the worst of the cold, but big enough to let in some light and breeze in the summer.

She was in Alaska, for sure. God, what was she doing here?

Kaylie tossed the clean clothes on the sink and unzipped her jacket, dropping it on the floor. She tugged all her layers off, including the light blue sweater that had felt so safe this morning when she'd put it on. She stared grimly at her black lace bra, so utterly feminine, exactly the kind of bra that her mother had always considered frivolous and completely impractical. Which it was. Which was why that was the only style Kaylie ever wore.

She should never have come to Alaska. She didn't belong here. She couldn't handle this. Kaylie gripped the edge of the sink. Her hands dug into the wood as she fought against the urge to curl into a ball and cry.

After a minute, Kaylie lifted her head and looked at herself in the mirror. Her eyes were wide and scared, with dark circles beneath. Her hair was tangled and flattened from her wool hat. There was dirt caked on her cheeks.

Kaylie rubbed her hand over her chin, and the streaks of mud didn't come off.

She tried again, then realized she had smudges all over her neck. She turned on the water, and wet her hands...and saw her hands were covered as well.

Stunned, Kaylie stared as the water ran over her hands, turning pink as it swirled in the basin.

Not dirt.

Sara's blood.

"Oh, God." Kaylie grabbed a bar of soap and began to scrub her hands. But the blood was dried, stuck to her skin. "Get off!" She rubbed frantically, but the blackened crust wouldn't come off. Her lungs constricted and she couldn't breathe. "I can't—"

The door slammed open, and Cort stood behind her,

wearing a T-shirt and jeans.

The tears burst free at the sight of Cort, and Kaylie held up her hands to him. "I can't get it off—"

"I got it." Cort took her hands and held them under the water, his grip warm and strong. "Take a deep breath, Kaylie. It's okay."

"It's not. It won't be." She leaned her head against his shoulder, closing her eyes as he washed her hands roughly and efficiently. His muscles flexed beneath her cheek, his skin hot through his shirt. Warm. Alive. "Sara's dead," she whispered. "My parents. My brother. They're all gone. The blood—" Sobs broke free again, and she couldn't stop the trembling.

"I know. I know, babe." He pulled her hands out from under the water and grabbed a washcloth. He turned her toward him and began to wash her face and neck.

His eyes were troubled, his mouth grim. But his hands were gentle where he touched her, gently holding her face still while he scrubbed. His gaze flicked toward hers, and he held contact for a moment, making her want to fall into those brown depths and forget everything. To simply disappear into the energy that was him. "You have to let them go," he said. "There's nothing you can do to bring them back—"

"No." A deep ache pounded at Kaylie's chest and her legs felt like they were too weak to support her. "I can't. Did you see Sara? And Jackson? His throat—" She bent over, clutching her stomach. "I—"

Cort's arms were suddenly around her, warm and strong, pulling her against his solid body. Kaylie fell into him, the sobs coming hard, the memories—

"I know." Cort's whisper was soft, his hand in her hair, crushing her against him. "It sucks. Goddamn, it sucks."

Kaylie heard his grief in the raw tone of his voice and realized his body was shaking as well. She looked up and saw a rim of red around his eyes, shadows in the hollows of his whiskered cheeks. "You know," she whispered, knowing with absolute certainty that he did. He understood the grief consuming her.

"Yeah." He cupped her face, staring down at her, his grip so tight it was almost as desperate as she felt. She could feel his heart beating against her nearly bare breasts, the rise of his chest as he breathed, the heat of his body warming the deathly chill from hers.

For the first time in forever, she suddenly didn't feel quite as alone.

In her suffering, she had company. Someone who knew. Who understood. Who shared her pain. It had been so long since the dark cavern surrounding her heart had lessened, since she hadn't felt consumed by the loneliness, but with Cort holding her...there was a flicker of light in the darkness trying to take her. "Cort—"

He cleared his throat. "I gotta go check the chili." He dropped his hands from her face and stood up to go, pulling away from her.

Without his touch, the air felt cold and the anguish returned full force. Kaylie caught his arm. "Don't go—" She stopped, not sure what to say, what to ask for. All she knew was that she didn't want him to leave, and she didn't want him to stop holding her.

Cort turned back to her, and a muscle ticked in his cheek.

For a moment, they simply stared at each other. She raised her arms. "Hold me," she whispered. "Please."

He hesitated for a second, and then his hand snaked out and he shackled her wrist. He yanked once, and she tumbled into him. Their bodies smacked hard as he caught her around the waist, his hands hot on her bare back.

She threw her arms around his neck and sagged into him. He wrapped his arms around her, holding her tightly against him. With only her bra and his T-shirt between them, the heat of his body was like a furnace, numbing her pain.

His name slipped out in a whisper, and she pressed her cheek against his chest. She focused on his masculine scent. She took solace in the feel of another human's touch, in the safety of being held in arms powerful enough to ward off the grief trying to overtake her.

His hand tunneled in her hair, and he buried his face in the curve of her neck, his body shaking against hers.

"Cort—" She started to lift her head to look at him, to see if he was crying, but he tightened his grip on her head, forcing her face back to his chest, refusing to allow her to look at him.

Keeping her out.

Isolating her.

She realized he wasn't a partner in her grief. She was alone, still alone, always alone.

All the anguish came cascading back. Raw loneliness surged again, and she shoved away from him as sobs tore at her throat. She couldn't deal with being held by him when the sense of intimacy was nothing but an illusion. "Leave me alone."

Kaylie whirled away from him, keeping her head ducked. She didn't want to look at him. She needed space to find her equilibrium again and rebuild her foundation.

"Damn it, Kaylie." Cort grabbed her arm and spun her back toward him.

She held up her hands to block him, her vision blurred by the tears streaming down her face. "Don't—"

His arms snapped around her and he hauled her against him even as she fought his grip. "No! Leave me alone—"

His mouth descended on hers.

Not a gentle kiss.

A kiss of desperation and grief and need. Of the need to control something. Of raw human passion for life, for death, for the touch of another human being.

And it broke her.

SNEAK PEEK: PRINCE CHARMING CAN WAIT

EVER AFTER
Available Now

Clouds were thick in the sky, blocking the moon. The lake and the woods were dark, swallowing up light and life, like a soothing blanket of nothingness coating the night. Emma needed to get away from the world she didn't belong to, the one that held no place for her. Tears were thick in her throat, her eyes stinging as she ran. The stones were wet from the rain earlier in the day, and the cool dampness sent chills through her.

She reached the dock and leapt out onto the damp wood. Her foot slipped, and she yelped as she lost her balance—

Strong hands shot out and grabbed her around the waist, catching her before she fell into the water. Shrieking in surprise, she jerked free, twisting out of range. The evasive move sent her off balance again, her feet went out from under her, and she was falling—

And again, someone grabbed her. "Hey," a low voice said. "I'm not going to hurt you."

Emma froze at the sound of the voice she knew so well, the one that had haunted her for so many sleepless nights. The voice she thought she'd never hear again, because he'd been gone for so long. "Harlan?"

"Yeah."

Emma spun around in his grasp, and her breath caught as she saw his shadowed face. His eyes were dark and hooded in the filtered light, his cheek bones more prominent than they had been the last time she'd seen him. Heavy stubble framed his face, and his hair was long and ragged around the base of his neck. He was leaner than she remembered, but his muscles were more defined, straining at his tee shirt. He looked grungy and real, a man who lived by the earth every day of his life. He exuded pure strength and raw appeal that ignited something deep within her. She instinctively leaned toward him, into the strength that emanated from him. His hands felt hot and dangerous where they clasped her hips, but she had no urge to push him away.

Damn him. After not seeing him for nearly a year, he still affected her beyond reason.

"You're back," she managed.

"Yeah."

Again, the one word answer. He had never said much more than that to her, but she'd seen him watching her intently on countless occasions, his piercing blue eyes roiling with so much unspoken emotion and turbulence. She managed a small smile, trying to hide the intensity of her reaction to seeing him. "Astrid didn't mention you would be here."

"She doesn't know." Again, he fell silent, but he raised one hand and lifted a lock of her hair, thumbing it gently. "Like silk," he said softly. "Just as I always thought it would feel."

Her heart began to pound now. There was no way to stop it, not when she was so close to him, not when she could feel his hands on her, a touch she'd craved since the first time she'd seen him. It had been two years ago, the day she'd walked back into her life in Birch Crossing. He had been leaning against the deli counter in Wright's, his arms folded over his chest, his piercing blue eyes watching her so intently.

And now he was here, in these woods, holding onto her.

His grip was strong, but his touch was gentle in her hair as he filtered the strands through his fingers. "You've thought about my hair before?" she asked. Ridiculous question, but it tumbled out anyway. And she wanted to know. Had he really thought about her before? Was she not alone in the way her mind had wandered to him so many nights when she hadn't been able to sleep?

His gaze met hers, and for a second, heat seemed to explode between them. Then he dropped his hands and stepped back. The loss of his touch was like ice cold water drenching her, and she had to hug herself to keep from reaching out for him.

"Tell Astrid I was here," he said. "I'm leaving again—"

"What?" She couldn't hold back the protest. "Already? Why?"

"I have a job."

That job. That mysterious job. He had never told Astrid, or anyone else in town, where he went when he disappeared. Sometimes, he was in town for months, playing at his real estate business, taking off for only a few days at a time. Other times, he was absent for longer. This last time, he'd been gone for almost a year, which was the longest that anyone could remember him being away. And he was leaving again already? "Astrid misses you," Emma said quickly, instinctively trying to give him a reason not to disappear again. "You can't leave without at least saying hi."

Harlan's gaze flickered to the house, and his mouth tightened. He made no move to join the celebration, and suddenly she realized that he felt the same way she did about invading that happy little world. He didn't belong to it any more than she did. Empathy tightened her chest, and she looked more carefully at the independent man who no one in town had ever been able to get close to. "You can stop by and see her tomorrow," she said softly.

He didn't move, and he didn't take his eyes off the house. "She's happy? Jason's good to her?"

Emma nodded. "He treasures her. They're so in love." She couldn't quite keep the ache out of her voice, and she saw Harlan look sharply at her.

"What's wrong?" he asked. "Why did you say it like that?"

"No, no, they're great. Really." She swallowed and pulled back her shoulders, refusing to let herself yearn for that which she did not want or need in her life. "She would kill me if she found out I let you leave town without seeing her. How long until you have to go?"

He shifted. "Forty-eight hours." The confession was reluctant.

"So, then, come back here tomorrow and see her," she said, relief rushing through her at the idea that he wasn't leaving town immediately. For at least two nights, she could sleep knowing that he was breathing the same air as she was.

"No, not here." He ran his hand through his hair, and she saw a dark bruise on the underside of his triceps. "You guys still go to Wright's in the morning for coffee?"

Emma's heart fluttered at his question. For a man who had held himself aloof, he seemed endearingly aware of what his sister did every day...and he knew that she was always there as well. "Yes. We'll be there at eight thirty."

He nodded. "Yeah, okay, I'll try to make it then." He glanced at her again, and just like before, heat seemed to rush through her—

Then he turned away, stealing that warmth from her before she'd had time to finish savoring it. "No." She grabbed his arm, her fingers sliding over his hard muscles. Shocked by the feel of his body beneath her palm, she jerked back, but not soon enough.

He froze under her touch, sucking in his breath. Slowly, he turned his head to look back at her. "No?"

"Don't try to make it tomorrow morning," she said quickly, trying to pretend her panic had been on Astrid's behalf, not her own. "You have to make it. Astrid needs to see you. She wants you to meet Rosie. She's happy, Harlan, but she needs her brother, too. Jason is her family, but so are you, and you know how she needs to be connected."

Harlan closed his eyes for a long moment, and she saw

emotions warring within him. For a man so stoic and aloof, he was fermenting with emotions in a way that she'd never seen before. She looked again at the bruise on his arm. "Are you okay, Harlan? What happened while you were gone?" There was no way to keep the concern out of her voice, no way to hide that her heart ached at the thought of him being hurt.

His eyes opened again. He said nothing, but he suddenly wrapped his hand around the back of her neck.

She stiffened, her heart pounding as he drew her close to him. "What are you doing?"

"I need this." Then he captured her mouth with his.

She had no time to be afraid, no time to fear. His kiss was too desperate for her to be afraid. It wasn't a kiss to seduce or dominate. It was a burning, aching need for connection, for humanity, for something to chase away the darkness hunting him...everything she needed in a kiss as well.

Her hands went instinctively to his chest, bracing, protecting, but at the same time, connecting. She kissed him back, needing the same touch that he did, desperate for that feeling of being wanted. She didn't know this man, and yet, on some level, she'd known him for so long. She'd seen his torment, she'd felt his isolation, and she'd witnessed his unfailing need to protect Astrid, even if he had never inserted himself fully into her life.

Somehow, Harlan's kiss wasn't a threat the way other men's were. He was leaving town, so he was no more than a shadow that would ease into her life and then disappear. He wouldn't try to take her, to trick her, to consume her. He wouldn't make promises and then betray them. All he wanted was the same thing she did, a break from the isolation that locked him down, a fragile whisper of human connection to fill the gaping hole in his heart.

"Emma!" Astrid's voice rang out in the night, shattering the moment. "Are you out here?"

Harlan broke the kiss, but he didn't move away, keeping

his lips against hers. One of his hands was tangled lightly in her hair, the other was locked around her waist. Somehow, he'd pulled them close, until her breasts were against his chest, their bodies melted together. It felt so right, but at the same time, a familiar anxiety began to build inside Emma at the intimacy.

"Do not fear me, sweet Emma," Harlan whispered against her lips. "I would only treasure what you give."

His voice was so soft and tender that her throat tightened. How she'd yearned for so many years, for a lifetime, for someone to speak to her like that…until she'd finally become smart enough to relinquish that dream. And now, here it was, in the form of a man who would disappear from her life in forty-eight hours, maybe never to return. Which was why it was okay, because she didn't have to worry that he would want more than she could give, or that she would give him more than she could afford. Maybe she didn't belong in the room of couples and families, but for this brief moment, she belonged out in the night, with a man who lived the same existence that she did.

"Emma?" Astrid's footsteps sounded on the deck, and Harlan released her.

"Don't tell her I was here," he said. "I'll come by Wright's in the morning. Now is not the time." Then, without a sound, he faded into the darkness, vanishing so quickly she almost wondered whether she'd imagined him.

STEPHANIE ROWE BIO

Four-time RITA® Award nominee and Golden Heart® Award winner Stephanie Rowe is a nationally bestselling author with more than twenty published books with major New York publishers such as Grand Central, HarperCollins, Harlequin, Dorchester and Sourcebooks.

She has received coveted starred reviews from Booklist and high praise from Publisher's Weekly, calling out her "... snappy patter, goofy good humor and enormous imagination... [a] genre-twister that will make readers...rabid for more." Stephanie's work has been nominated as YALSA Quick Pick for Reluctant Readers.

Stephanie writes romance (paranormal, contemporary and romantic suspense), teen fiction, middle grade fiction and motivational nonfiction.

A former attorney, Stephanie lives in Boston where she plays tennis, works out and is happily writing her next book. Want to learn more? Visit Stephanie online at one of the following hot spots:

www.stephanierowe.com

http://twitter.com/stephanierowe2

https://www.facebook.com/StephanieRoweAuthor

Select List of Other Books by Stephanie Rowe

(For a complete book list, please visit www.stephanierowe.com)

Paranormal Romance

The Order of the Blade Series
Darkness Awakened
Darkness Seduced
Darkness Surrendered
Forever in Darkness (Novella)
Darkness Reborn
Darkness Arisen
Darkness Unleashed
Inferno of Darkness
Darkness Possessed
Available 2014

The Soulfire Series
Kiss at Your Own Risk
Touch if You Dare
Hold Me if You Can

The Immortally Sexy Series
Date Me Baby, One More Time
Must Love Dragons
He Loves Me, He Loves Me Hot
Sex & the Immortal Bad Boy

Romantic Suspense

The Alaska Heat Series
Ice
Chill
Ghost
Available early 2014

Contemporary Romance

Ever After Series
No Knight Needed
Fairytale Not Required
Prince Charming Can Wait

The Knight Who Brought Chocolate
Available 2014

STAND ALONE NOVELS
Jingle This!

NONFICTION

The Feel Good Life

FOR TEENS

A GIRLFRIEND'S GUIDE TO BOYS SERIES
Putting Boys on the Ledge
Studying Boys
Who Needs Boys?
Smart Boys & Fast Girls

STAND ALONE NOVELS
The Fake Boyfriend Experiment

FOR PRE-TEENS

THE FORGOTTEN SERIES
Penelope Moonswoggle, The Girl Who Could Not Ride a Dragon
Penelope Moonswoggle & the Accidental Doppelganger
Release Date TBD

Made in United States
North Haven, CT
08 June 2022

19993301R00114